THE C[illegible]

Adam Kolczynski wa[illegible] f
Waltham Forest in October, 198[illegible]. He read Biochemistry at St Peter's College, Oxford, and Modern History at St Benet's Hall. A third-generation Pole, he is fortunate to be bilingual and retains a strong cultural affinity with the country of his grandparents' birth. He divides his time between London, Warsaw and Jávea, Spain. *The Oxford Virus* is his first novel.

THE OXFORD VIRUS

ADAM KOLCZYNSKI

POLYBIUS BOOKS
- London -

POLYBIUS BOOKS

Published in Great Britain in 2010 by Polybius Books

A CIP catalogue record for this book
is available from the British Library

ISBN 978-0-9565880-0-5

Typeset in Spectrum by Palimpsest Book Production Ltd,
Falkirk, Stirlingshire.

Printed and bound in Great Britain by CPI Cox & Wyman, Reading, RG1 8EX.

Polybius Books
124 Corringway
London
W5 3HA

www.polybiusbooks.com

For Maryla Winter, née Porembińska

'. . . science gathers knowledge faster than society gathers wisdom.'

Isaac Asimov

PART ONE

CHAPTER ONE

'His findings were frightening in their simplicity, incalculable in their implications. Precious.'

'Everything in order?' rasped the voice through the receiver.

On another day, Dr. Lomana Olembé might have retorted, 'as much as it *can* be in a game of chance.' But he opted for the plainest of affirmatives: a single 'yes'.

He pictured the rough-hewn Chairman, pacing his kitchen, Bluetooth headset clipped to one ear. In a little over thirty-six hours, Professor Trent would be attending that all-important business lunch. To sell, or not to sell? – the tireless question.

Olembé was an entirely different specimen. He did not stalk the corridors of power. Never had; never would. Insomnia was an occupational hazard. Seldom would a week pass by without some obstacle to lucid thought: a throbbing in his spine; an animal rights protest; a power surge. As the Cameroonian replaced his handset and jerked the curtains into an ill-fitting overlap across the bedroom window, he found himself smouldering at the injustice of it all.

Outrage, loneliness, regret – Olembé had tasted all three, each inflamed by his wife's agonising death. He'd resolved to stifle these gnawings by immersing himself in his work; by beaming light into the black, blank reaches of cancer research. Colleagues had done all they could to assuage his torment. So far, with little success.

The clock on his bedside table bleeped twice. 23:30 – eight hours to go. He bit into his lower lip, hard and deep, the metallic tang intensifying. Then came the fear.

*

On 3rd January 2010, Lorenex Biotherapeutics had announced its completion of a cancer-targeting virus: *Vaccinia* LX-427. For years, the corporation had sought to justify its heavy investment in the drug, while also proving that there was substance in its motto, 'SKILL WITH SERENDIPITY'. In animal trials, the virus had outshone an array of gold standard treatments. Of the forty lab mice afflicted with brain tumours, sixty percent had recovered within a month. The remainder had shown appreciable signs of improvement, only to succumb to lethal brain-stem compression as the cancer took hold. In his capacity as Chief Scientific Officer, Olembé was relieved that none of the rodents had exhibited the balding, lethargy and general malaise he might have expected with chemo-therapy. His findings were frightening in their simplicity, incalculable in their implications. Precious.

After prolonged appraisal, the Medicines and Healthcare

products Regulatory Agency (MHRA) had sanctioned a phase one clinical trial. The May study would focus on *Vaccinia's* safety and tolerability profile in no fewer than fifty healthy volunteers. It would be conducted at the Churchill Hospital, Headington, Oxford.

Before that came Delia Holdenby.

The forty-year-old English teacher had been diagnosed with a malignant tumour in her oesophagus. Powerless to curb its growth, consultant oncologists had resigned themselves to defeat within a fortnight. Olembé's first contact with Delia had come through the mysterious physicality of cyberspace. His videophone had vibrated twice as he rubbed his hands beneath a dryer in the staff toilets. Not that it mattered precisely where he took the call or how he looked – his phone was set to one-way video transmission, displaying but not sending.

Olembé peered at the screen. Despite its dubious graphics, his eyes were drawn to a rectangle of light enlivening a matt-walled room. A plasma TV, perhaps? The walls were painted the same inoffensive pink as the doors. Accent lighting lent a sparkle to the myriad rows of glass and porcelain. His patient-to-be sat numbly in an armchair, barely registering the affections of her long-haired tortoiseshell. The cat purred contentedly at her ankles, one eyelid sutured, the other retracted to reveal a saffron iris. Delia's were limpid green. What remained of her hair had been coaxed into a headscarf, sharp chin tucked retiringly into a shawl. Her modesty was preserved by a white bathrobe. She looked haggard and almost old, tugging at life like a desperate child to its mother's hemline.

After an initial burst of energy, Delia weakened before his eyes. Tightening her bathrobe cord, she nodded in an indeterminate direction – a heavy, stoical nod. The grainy picture lurched, then wobbled, as the videophone changed hands. Her fleshless figure receded into the depths of the lounge to be replaced, seconds later, by the porcine one of Richard Holdenby.

With his bulging eyes and ungainly auburn hair, Holdenby exuded neither subtlety nor sophistication. Yet his manners were polished. One arm akimbo, he spoke with a calm authority, never ducking the videophone's virtual gaze. His voice was deep and melodious, with a hint of self-indulgence in his clipped consonants and broad As. Public school snoot, thought Olembé. And proud of it.

What Olembé did not know was that the ghostwriter's relations with his clients had soured of late. As Delia's needs mounted, background research became difficult, client taping sessions impossible. A few – the merciful few – were willing to wait, presumably swayed by the excellence of his pedigree. But the rest grew tired of multiple delays. A contract was a contract, and their stories pined for publication. Prizing immediacy over inclusivity, they turned their attentions elsewhere. Accustomed to having his 'co-authorship' acknowledged on the covers of ghosted books, Holdenby felt slighted like never before.

Yet he refused to capitulate. Surrender was alien to him, inaction unthinkable. At life's nadir, he resolved to reclaim control: he would trawl the web for an elusive cure.

One foggy evening in early March, his waning hopes were reinvigorated. Having ravaged his third energy bar in as many hours, Holdenby had been about to remove yet another unhelpful link from Favorites, log off, lock the study door, let the cat out, set the burglar alarm, and join his wife upstairs.

Something made him stop.

www.lorenex-bio.com was the 9th of 26,400 Google links containing the word 'virotherapy'. More to the point, it was part of a tiny cluster of websites intelligible even to a layman like himself. The red LED of his iFeel mouse had pulsed with each frantic flick of the scroll wheel:

> *'The virus. An invisible menace. The ever-changing bane of mankind. The suffering wrought by Ebola – the culprit behind haemorrhagic fever – bolsters this pervasive perception. But have we, in our indignation, been blinded to something so sensational as to shake the very fabric of modern medicine? Supposing viruses could be bio-engineered to our benefit. Supposing these unlikely saviours could be unleashed upon a tumour, weeks away from encroaching upon vital organs. What if this newly 'infected' tumour could itself become a virus factory, sending forth wave upon wave of destruction towards nearby carcinomas[1]? All this, whilst leaving healthy cells intact . . .*

This is our vision, my friends, and by working in concord, oncolytic[2] virotherapy can – and surely will – inch towards the medicine cabinet.

[1] carcinoma: a malignant cancer arising from tissues that line or cover body organs. The growth tends to infiltrate surrounding tissues and spread to distant regions via lymphatic or blood vessels. A carcinoma is firm, irregular and nodular, with a well-defined border.

[2] oncolytic: onco – 'tumour', from Greek onkos, 'mass, swelling'. lytic – 'killing', from Greek lysis, 'a loosening or dissolution'.

Passing over standard pleasantries, Holdenby had pressed for an immediate consultation.

'We're based in Cheltenham,' explained Dr. Olembé, studying his fingernails with undue interest. 'The Wilburn Building, fourth floor. We have lifts, you understand, but the corridors are fairly tedious.'

'Your point being . . . '

'That your wife might struggle without a wheelchair.'

'Struggle?' gasped Holdenby, arching a ginger eyebrow. 'Delia's got no conception of the word! Ever since that beastly endoscopy, she can barely keep down solids. Until now, her response has been admirable: "Damn gullet! Chuck it in the blender, would you dear, and let's have it puréed." That's Delia in a nutshell.' He lowered his voice. 'Death is so mundane, Doctor. Millions do it daily. Some expire in a flash; others hang around to write sprawling memoirs. I don't pretend to know what fate has in store for my wife, but I know *this* much: she won't go down without a fight.'

Olembé sighed, a little too affectedly. 'I'll do all I can, Mr. Holdenby. It is her right and privilege.' His hooded eyes departed the videophone screen. 'I have a slot at twelve-fifteen next Tuesday.'

'March 23rd?'

'Correct. And be sure to send me her CT scans by first class mail. Got to know what I'm dealing with, you see.'

Holdenby tapped a nearby manila envelope. 'Will do, Doctor. Tuesday it is.'

In the empty lounge his voice sounded thin and hollow. Upstairs a floorboard creaked – Delia was settling down to sleep.

CHAPTER TWO

'"There is hope for us. Hope for us yet." But the obliqueness of his glance was unmistakable.'

A clear run along the A40 brought the Cotswolds into view a full twenty minutes ahead of schedule. Pastures rose steeply into tramlined oat fields. Broken by limestone outcrops, the vista was further punctuated by rows of wind turbines, blades swishing frenziedly. All the while, Delia sat beside her husband, chin propped on her palm, expression indecipherable.

By midday, the maroon Audi R8 found itself opposite Cheltenham Spa railway station. The sky remained a formless pall of grey, unmarred by the recent winds. Having fed the pay-and-display machine to its four-hour limit, the couple lumbered past a taxi rank and approached the towering gates of Savinaud Place.

The biomedical park was a mélange of specialist conference suites, amenity buildings and sunken seating areas. Light swirled in eddies across a typically sparse Zen garden, raked white gravel suggestive of a purling brook. The Wilburn Building reared high over the seventy-acre site, blue-tinted glass and recessed upper stories lending a touch of lightness to its imposing shell. The revolving doors hung on a central shaft. Beside them stood an intercom station. After a moment's readjustment, Holdenby pressed the red button to the right of its flush-mounted microphone.

'Mrs. Holdenby?' crackled a honeyed voice.

Delia confirmed her identity with a huff of irritation.

'The start-up sensors are being serviced today,' added the switchboard operator. 'Give us a sec and I'll open the separate entrance on your left.'

A heartening click issued from the door. Leaning his portly frame against it, Holdenby guided his wife over the threshold and into a cavernous, six-storey atrium.

They were greeted at reception by what transpired to be Lorenex's Chief Technologist, Dr. Turner. The man was barely thirty, Delia presumed, but already had an ingrained sense of his own inestimable worth. Mumbling something about an 'east wing' and a 'long walk', he escorted them out of the atrium and through a side door bearing a foamboard *Authorised Personnel Only* sign. Somewhat riled by this perfunctory welcome, the couple began their synchronised trudge through a warren of dustless corridors. Planted in Dr. Turner's right hand was a thin plastic card. This he swiped through a succession of security doors, footsteps echoing through the stillness. Delia channelled her meagre weight through a forearm crutch, chin held high, arm nestled in the crook of her husband's elbow. Not a word was spoken as the elevator rose to the fourth floor with a hydraulic moan, or as its doors opened at their destination with an insistent ping.

Having ushered the couple through a final pair of doors, the technologist handed them each a lab coat. 'For your protection!' he boomed. 'Compulsory for all human traffic. Company policy.'

'Company policy indeed,' mouthed Holdenby, attending to his wife's upturned collar. He took exception to the phrase, 'human traffic' – it was as impersonal as the welcome. Running a freckled hand through his hair, he wondered just what 'non-human traffic' might entail.

They entered the bowels of the research facility: an array of workbenches and gleaming countertops. Catching her breath, Delia detected a faint yet familiar tang; the very scent that had wafted in and out of the Truelove 5F Ward during those four dismal days at the John Radcliffe Hospital. Synthetic raspberries. Virkon. Now, as then, she had Richard by her side.

A network of overhead lighting heightened the air of sterility. Natural rays might have flooded the facility had its clerestory windows not been obscured by plastic sheeting.

'Being resealed with silicone caulk,' clarified the technologist. 'Much more virologically hermetic and cuts our energy costs. Oh, and I suppose it lowers our carbon footprint,' he supplied with a ghost of a grin. A gratuitous, ill-timed grin.

They filed past a group of workers. Delia glanced nervously at the mousy-haired woman operating what she presumed to be a centrifuge. Having lifted its plastic cover, the gloved hands removed a tiny tapered vial from one of the numbered wells. Displaying phenomenal sleight of hand, they began to decant the colourless liquid, first drawing it up into a narrow pipette, then squeezing the rubber bulb into a beaker. As for what remained in the centrifuge tip, or its relevance to cancer research, lay comfortably outside Delia's orbit.

Turner motioned them down a stairway lit by low-bay lamps. 'Here we are,' he affirmed, divesting them of their lab coats in two grandiose sweeps. 'Unless he's absconded, Dr. Olembé should be through here.'

The office tier was awash with cubicles. Holdenby was convinced that Perspex, like that in the visor of his old motorbike helmet, had provided a cheaper surrogate to privacy glass. Rather than terminating at the ceiling tiles, each frameless screen extended as far as the ceiling deck. He put the nearest cubicle at a little over twelve metres squared. Graphs and diagrams covered two of its three walls. Black computer cables ran down the back of a cluttered Formica desk.

Having plumbed the depths of eloquence on Lorenex's website, Olembé had smacked of the archetypal activist: blustering, impassioned, obstinate. But the Holdenbys were greeted by a meek and unassuming medic. Olembé was bald except for wiry tussocks that sprouted vagrantly from behind each earlobe. A diffuse pinkness in the whites of his eyes hinted at a mild case of conjunctivitis, or an acute lack of sleep. Rounded features and sloping shoulders leant him more than a passing resemblance to a tubular bell. Proffering a bony hand, the doctor inclined his head, sighed fittingly, and beckoned the couple to sit.

'Make yourselves as comfortable as possible,' he began, transferring his tie-clip microphone to a breast pocket. 'I daresay we'll be here for quite some time. Your case, Mrs. Holdenby, is most intriguing. You'll be pleased to know that I've browsed through the radiologist's report.' He paused to slide his wireless keyboard into a space beneath the Formica desk. 'Put simply, we have a near infinite number of strategies and points of origin. I should like to guide you through my reasoning.'

The Holdenbys looked up expectantly, eyes riveted on those of the mahogany-skinned doctor.

'Let me be frank with you both – always the best policy, I find. There's no consensus on how best to administer oncolytic viruses. We simply aren't that far down the line, nor are . . .'

'We feared this,' broke in Holdenby, a shade pugnaciously. 'Seemed too good to be true.'

'Never fear, Mr. Holdenby – I was merely outlining the inherent challenges. To date, virotherapy has worked best when our virus is injected directly into the tumour. This is entirely impractical in your wife's case, as her oesophageal cancer has already spread to distant lymph nodes. Do you follow?'

The Holdenbys nodded, Delia rather more emphatically.

'So what we require is a form of infusion – intermittent or continuous – that can destroy her tumour regardless of how far it has metastasised. Intravenous administration could be our shortcut, as several lab mice will doubtless testify. The trick is to put the right virus in the right place;

to deliver it to the malignancy without sparking an immune reaction. The biggest obstacle lies in getting our virus past this first line of defence.'

'Antibodies?' probed Delia, pronouncing the word as if picking it up with tweezers.

'Precisely, Mrs. Holdenby.' Olembé was pleasantly surprised at this show of knowledge. 'The last thing we want is for your own antibodies to repel the therapy before it reaches its destination. Here at Lorenex, we've been exploring ways to bypass these frisky sentries. *Vaccinia*, used as a vaccine against smallpox, is already proficient in this. Why, you may ask? Put simply, the virus has the rare ability to coat itself with proteins, allowing it to cruise through the bloodstream in an undetected state. An extracellular envelope, if you like.'

Holdenby blinked twice. 'So it's been in the pipeline for years, right?'

'Indeed it has,' certified Olembé. 'The unmodified virus, to be precise. You'll forgive me for quoting my Oxford pharmacology tutor at this stage in proceedings: "Concepts are like oil – the further down the pipeline they move, the less of a pipe dream they become." Just one of his many pearls of wisdom.'

'Good one, good one,' conceded Holdenby, allowing himself a faint simper for the first time that afternoon. He knew good wordplay when he saw it.

But Delia seemed unconvinced. 'So when do immuno-suppressant drugs come into play, Doctor? Richard was reading up on them yesterday.'

'They don't,' countered Olembé, shaking his head sagely. 'By creating a stealth virus, the hope is that our cancer-fighting agent is rendered invisible to the immune system. Moreover, it's not in your interests for us to suppress your natural defences if we can avoid it. Doing so would heighten your susceptibility to a range of hospital superbugs.'

Delia jutted a quizzical underlip at the doctor. 'But what if I contract the very virus you'll be injecting into me?'

'Allow me to deconstruct the issue,' replied Olembé, folding his arms. 'Most vaccines use weakened forms of the virus being vaccinated against, agreed? The *Vaccinia* vaccine is a notable exception. While it protects against smallpox, it doesn't actually contain *Variola*, the smallpox virus.'

Holdenby cleared his throat. 'What *does* it contain?'

'It is closely related to the virus that causes cowpox – comparatively harmless as viruses go. Be advised that complications can and do arise in a tiny subset of patients. Approximately one in a million will develop a fatal response to the vaccination. Weak immune systems narrow these odds somewhat.'

'By how much?' asked Delia, coughing into a tissue.

'That's largely academic. I need you to understand that you won't be crossing swords with the *Vaccinia* vaccine. Not directly. In its place, I'll be administering a modified strain of *Vaccinia* uniquely suited to infecting tumours. Yes, their molecular biologies are related, but the latter owes its broad oncolytic spectrum to its ability to target the EGF-Receptor pathway. This pathway is mutated in a wide range of cancers. Yours happens to be one of them.'

'I suppose that's good, then?' presented Holdenby.

Olembé answered him with an elastic smile. 'The procedure should be virtually painless: peripheral IV lines connected to a rapid infuser. Not a scalpel in sight. You might consider hiring a carer to help yourselves through the tough first week at home. Either way, your wife will be hospitalised for forty-eight hours as a precaution. She'll be paid an inconvenience fee for time spent in the centre. Pay is conditional on the length and extent of participation, which in her case should be to the tune of three hundred pounds per day. Not that I'm enamoured of the idea.'

Holdenby stifled a cough. 'And why is that, Doctor?'

'You're quite entitled to ask. From one angle, it seems only reasonable that a trialist should be reimbursed for their time and exposure to unknown risks. Adverse events, we like to call them.'

'And the other angle?' pressed Delia.

'Paying participants might well distort their judgement. Give them nothing, and you ensure that their motivation lies only in the hope of recovery, or of making a genuine contribution to medical knowledge. Fear not, Mrs. Holdenby, for I speak only hypothetically. This brings us to a rather delicate point.' Indecision tinged his hooded eyes. 'By proceeding with this study, you forfeit the right to all further treatment. This includes palliative chemotherapy.'

'Yes, yes,' rebounded Delia, fuelled by little more than adrenaline. 'That's exactly what the Greek guy said at the JR! With NHS rationing being what it is, I expect it doesn't pay to waste valuable resources on a patient who's opted for vanguard therapy.'

'No, no, nothing like that,' said Olembé with renewed equanimity. 'It's purely to ensure that the chemotherapy drugs don't interfere with our live virus; don't lower its potency, if you like. Remember, Mrs. Holdenby, that if you were to continue with chemotherapy alongside virotherapy and *still* exhibited tumour regression, I'd be unable to ascertain which treatment you'd responded to.' He chuckled. 'That wouldn't be very scientific, now, would it? My peers would have a field-day!'

But Delia was impervious to wit. Taut as a mannequin, her green eyes settled on a photograph blu-tacked to the Perspex. A swarthy countenance, brow-ridges prominent, almond eyes beaming in tandem with the lips. The smile – that culture-transcending touchstone, enough to distinguish genuine emotion from its contrived counterpart.

Sentiments rekindled.

Her first day at primary school – flaxen-haired, garbed in a red tie and grey flannel skirt, satchel held aloft with gusto. Or that panoramic photo overlooking the digital organ console at No. 2 London Road, Oxford. Hand-beaded and silken, her bridal gown appeared luminous against the modern glass frontage of St Columba's United Reformed Church. Incessant rainfall. A youthful crowd of confetti-hurlers. Back then, her face had been stenciled only by lines of frivolous humour. Now it was pallid and beseeching. Vulnerable.

Rumpling her brow, Delia willed her eyes away from the swarthy headshot. She leaned towards Olembé, orbs hollow in their caverns.

'Tell me, Doctor . . . do you think I'll make it?'

'We're quietly optimistic,' replied Olembé unflinchingly, 'though let me be square with you, Mrs. Holdenby. This is no silver bullet, you understand. Not *just* yet. Success depends on the highly specific interaction between virus and tumour. Contrary to what those laggards in Minnesota would have us believe, our studies suggest that the initial tumour volume is key in shaping the outcome of virotherapy. As counterintuitive as it may seem, there appears to be a correlation between the size of the tumour and the rate of virus-tumour interactions. The result is a higher pool of infected tumour cells, each with the capacity to generate new virus particles. These fuse with nearby tumours, halting their replication and hastening their death. Put differently,' he added, 'the sicker you are, the greater your chances of recovery.'

Holdenby leaned in closer. 'But it's still a case of ifs, buts and maybes?'

'Inevitably,' conceded Olembé. 'We're in the process of parameter estimation, you understand, but assuming our virus is administered over the next fortnight, I'm hoping the cancer will have stabilised by late April. With the capacity to deliver multiple therapeutic payloads, I expect a partial response within six weeks. By week eight, the treatment should be paying clear dividends. By week eleven, if all goes well, the tumour shrinkage should be visible through CT, MRI, or PET technology. Complete tumour regression should occur within thirty weeks, assuming of course that . . .'

But Olembé wilted before he could complete the thread. He shrank back from his clients; and he knew why. Holdenby's gesture of comfort to his wife – the tender clasping of an ashen hand – had scorched a fragile spirit. *His* spirit. A festering sore, first inflicted on that fateful spring morning. A wound unmoved by weeks of sympathetic counselling.

Mballa . . .

Profoundly shaken, Olembé snatched at the cool, dry air flooding the cubicle through a linear slot diffuser. He heard his grandfather's voice, smooth as an undulating sea: 'People gather logs to build bridges they never cross, Lomana. Anticipate everything but do not agonise, 'cos today is the tomorrow we worried about yesterday.'

With a prophetic sigh, Olembé broke the stiffening silence. 'There is hope for us. Hope for us yet.' But the obliqueness of his glance was unmistakable.

*

Nine days on, Olembé was poised for the simplest procedure of his career. Technically undemanding, its outcome was nonetheless shrouded in doubt. All too aware of this glaring paradox, the MHRA had granted him special dispensation to administer his virus in the grounds of the Churchill Hospital, Oxford. Specialist staff at the nearby John Radcliffe had been placed on standby. Two clinical immunologists, a consultant oesophago-gastric surgeon and an Associate Professor of Infectious Diseases would be within hailing distance in the event of snags and hitches.

'SKILL WITH SERENDIPITY'.

Olembé arrived in his metallic-orange Honda Elysion with forty minutes to spare. The morning sky was aglow with crimson and saffron, vivid as the rind of a grapefruit. He slid open the minivan door and gathered his briefcase with an unconvincing stab at nonchalance. Locking the vehicle, he made his way across the deserted car park, dew droplets shimmering on the asphalt, free arm dangling like an Iberian ham leg.

To his left lay a building site. In a little over two hours, that dormant welter of concrete mixers and Caterpillar 966Hs would throb into life, primed to perform their respective roles in the construction of a new cancer centre. Actors awaiting direction. Beyond the fairways of Southfield Golf Course sprawled historic Oxford, turrets and sandstone walls set against a cyclorama of countryside. To his right loomed the Radcliffe's white-tiled silhouette.

Olembé entered the timeless limbo of the Minor Procedures

Unit. The outside world seemed muffled, distant. Scrubbing-in with customary precision, he pondered the enormity of the chasm – chemical and physiological – separating mouse from human. Limited funding and relentless anti-vivisection campaigns had left his team with no other species on which to test their hypothesis. All hope now rested on a few recovered rodents. And still the question remained: what was to stop Delia Holdenby from being that one anomalous mouse, silently condemned to suffer a fatal immune reaction in the final week of trials? Seldom had a human trial been terminated on account of a drug's impotency. Hyperpotency was a quite different matter.

Olembé took a cursory glance at the antechamber calendar: Thursday, 1st April, 2010. The digital clock read 07:25. Whatever the outcome of the next thirty minutes, *that* date would always be seared into his consciousness. But who, in the event of a foul-up, would be branded 'The Fool' by a Board of Directors headed by the overbearing Professor T. Trent: eighty percent shareholder, Founder Member and Executive Chairman? Or in the dozens of e-journals that betrayed their truths, at the click of a mouse, to that gaggle of academics and corporate gurus? Would the epithet be applied to his own tireless workers for placing undue faith in a drug that was decades away from routine adoption by the NHS? Or would the greatest vitriol be reserved for that faceless naysayer, conventional medicine, for maintaining that nothing more could be done for Delia Holdenby and so many others?

Racked by a pounding nausea, Olembé donned his latex gloves and spinach-green gown. He reached for a striped bouffant cap, its elastic rim ensuring a snug fit with the back of his scalp. Throat constricted, he opened the antechamber doors. He stood at the edge of the sterile field, pulse racing.

The air was dry, the suite bright and austere. Ceiling-to-floor ventilation delivered a powerful airstream over the procedure table. All surfaces were coated with indium tin oxide, its antistatic properties explaining the absence of lint and dust. Two young Filipino nurses wheeled in a covered cart from the reprocessing area. Pausing to acknowledge him, they removed the dustcloth to reveal a colourless fluid bag.

Vaccinia.

His virus. His hope.

Delia's attire consisted of a baby blue hospital smock, her thin shins sleeved in magnolia compression stockings. A flowmeter delivered sweet-smelling laughing gas into each nostril. This would be titrated incrementally until a suitable O_2 to N_2O ratio was reached. Though the depth of sedation would wax and wane, she would remain clinically conscious throughout the procedure. There would be a vague impression of euphoric drift; a partial dissociation of pain; some transient paraesthesia of the limbs. In view of her self-confessed needle phobia, all three were highly desirable. A peripheral IV catheter would be secured to Delia's arm via an adhesive dressing. An inflatable cuff would girdle the fluid bag, and in so doing, force its viral contents into his supine patient.

All the while, he would wield complete control.

He, and he alone.

CHAPTER THREE

'"Brace yourself for a Russian doll: a surprise within a surprise."'

A fiery-eyed signet ring glistened on the crooked fourth finger. With an absent-mindedness that only Easter Vac could induce, the same finger rhythmically tapped the concave edge of the wireless mouse. Its owner was, in his own words, 'sinking fast into the quicksands of the morning's creative inertia, no?'

If the truth be told, Konstantin Vadimovich Zolotov had an almost clinical need for expanse. Having spent an unscheduled night in an airing cupboard as a small boy, the Russian couldn't abide the asphyxiating thought of being immured between floorboards – a neurosis kindled by that medley of vague clatter, muffled conversation and periphonic blare issuing so relentlessly at the whim of its creators. For these reasons alone, Zolotov had acquired a mortgage on an upmarket Summertown penthouse.

Tanley Court – variously christened his 'citadel', 'eyrie' or 'boiler room' – was a 1970s conception. Five-storey, with beige wirecut brickwork, the building was conveniently withdrawn from the tumult of Banbury Road. From his teak-decked roof terrace, over the boughs of a giant sycamore, he could see Oxford's tallest edifice: the Church of St Mary the Virgin. A life-affirming walk through leafy Summertown, past the twin temptations of the *Eagle and Child* and the *Lamb and Flag*, brought him to the Randolph's Victorian Gothic façade. Endowed with all the quietude of a private dwelling, its restaurant was run with an exactitude to rival the most elaborate Burns Night. The Châteaubriand steak was something of a speciality. Tenderloin aside, the consummate platter pulsed with sprouting broccoli, prosciutto-enswathed asparagus tips and an unlikely sextet of tempura-battered porta-bellinis. Julienned zucchini, drizzled with tarragon-infused olive oil, were thrown in for good measure.

If his dining colleague happened to be female, Zolotov found himself yielding to the offer of a 'shared' dessert. But what began as an exercise in temperance swiftly became a demonstration of mutual greed, as fork and spoon vied for a loganberry panna cotta. It was the woman who won. Invariably. Blithe of mind – if not in body – he would trade the adjoining Morse Bar for the promise of a vacant taxi. And providing the Faculty Finance Office agreed to subsidise his gluttony – or better still, incorporated it into end-of-year expenses – the epicure could be assured of guiltless slumber.

*

Back in the early eighties, Zolotov had received the opulence of Clapperton's main quadrangle with as much awe as incredulity. Faltering along the cobblestones of Logic Lane on his way to matriculation, mortarboard at the ready, he was buffeted by the rawhide mallet of honour; the pangs of insignificance. Beyond the Sheldonian's cupola, he began to witness his new world in oppressive beiges, arsenic greys, pernicious greens. His kite-shaped room was heated by two awry pipes, painted brown in defiance of the laws of physics. Mildew was rampant. Much as he pined for the admiration of his mentors, the doubts lingered: what could he, a twenty-six-year-old defector from the browbeaten USSR, offer the oldest university in the Anglosphere?

'Bedazzled by trepidation' – the words of Zolotov's history tutor as he prepared to declaim his maiden essay. Equally galling was the nickname, 'Konny Come Lately', an allusion to his mature student status.

Two events changed that.

The first – his fortuitous discovery of William Hazlitt's *Table Talk* in one of the Bodleian's many forsaken nooks. He grew to cherish the heartening caveats of Essay 31, 'On the Knowledge of Character', 1822:

> *'Modesty is the lowest of the virtues, and is a real confession of the deficiency it indicates. He who undervalues himself is justly undervalued by others. Whatever good properties he may possess are in fact neutralised by a cold rheum running through his veins, taking away the zest of his pretensions, the pith and marrow of his performance.'*

The second, more abiding instalment – a drunken vignette by a fellow student at Formal Hall.

'See those copper pipes snaking their way so concertedly from the Senior Common Room? Capital! Now picture the gigatonnes of virus-laden sludge rotting away at the local sewage plant.'

Zolotov's steak knife had hovered ambivalently over his stilton-bedaubed veal escalope. But he dared not interrupt.

'See the Master replenishing the Dean's glass with Mercurey Clos L'Eveque? Witness the studied smirks that follow each hood adjustment of their scarlet, silk-lined convocation habits? Next time you feel unusually worthless, picture them straining on a mummified bolus of impacted turd!'

A First Class Honours degree later – not mentioning the small matter of an M.Phil, a D.Phil and a paid sabbatical – the scion of ennobled Ataman Cossacks had crafted a comeback: 'Konny Leave Tardily.' By 2006, he was Professor Zolotov, Head of Russian and East European Studies; Senior Research Fellow at Clapperton College; *ex officio* Chairman of the Oxford University Vodka Society. He basked in his hard-earned laurels. And by early 2007, the last of the taunters had departed.

*

Zolotov had spent the morning in Flat 17B. Swivelling on an air-grid office chair, foam buds plugged firmly in his ears, he soaked up the familiar sounds of a Cossack folk dance. There was something infectious about the reedy timbre of the Saratovskaya garmonika; the wailing jaleika; the plectrum-strummed alto balalaika; the zither-like gusli. A marriage of symphonic precision and unabashed abandon, forged in the flames of perpetual strife. *Komandyr nash bravy* had been purchased for a mere seventy-nine pence. Suffice to say, it had cemented its place at the top of his iTunes playlist.

Dr. Rena Figueroa, Zolotov's research associate, sat cross-legged on one of the four leather sofas beside the electric feature fire. Her hair was russet, she wore no make-up; yet there was something appealingly Latin in her features, her olive complexion, her pronounced hips. She was skimming Professor Belmont's high-handed rebuttal of a recent Zolotov article entitled 'Catastroika: Plutocracy from Chaos, 1985-1991'. His orders. His bugbear.

Figueroa's upbringing was as exotic as her extraction. Born on the slopes of the Aconquija mountains to a local engineer and a Russian expatriate novelist, her family had migrated to Buenos Aires. Their decision was swiftly vindicated. By early 1985, the unshakable unit had acclimatised to Apartamiento 47A, a two-bedroom affair wedged between the inner floors of a ten-storey tower block. Its shingled turrets reared high over the exquisitely landscaped Barrancas de Belgrano. Sculptures and sidewalk cafés speckled the promenade. Brown Picazuro pigeons perched on telegraph wires like hats on clothes lines. Tango dancers enthralled pedestrians with an array of *sacadas*, their non-verbal dialogue conducted against the backcloth of a tango ensemble: strings; bandoneón trio; piano.

Within seven months, her mother's latest title had been dramatised under the pseudonym Y. J. Passarella. Even more meteoric was her father's emergence. Just two years after perfecting his industrial prototype, more than a dozen technology patents had been filed from the completion of Ramón Figueroa's centrifugal compressor. Originally intended for air separation plants, a catalogue of applications had surfaced: in diesel engine turbochargers, in pressurized aircraft to provide atmospheric pressure at high altitudes; in all fields of manufacturing to supply compressed air for pneumatic tools. Flush with cash, Ramón had made it his mission to bankroll his daughter's education.

Oxford she augured. Oxford she clinched. Her entry was secured after three years at the prestigious *Pontificia Universidad Católica Argentina*. Supplied with English from her worldly father and Russian from her Moscow-born mother, Figueroa soon found herself studying for a D. Phil in Soviet Historiography at Clapperton College. A Junior Research Fellowship had followed. With the dustcloud of newfound responsibility threatening to choke her, Figueroa had wasted little time in bidding farewell to the cult of *mañana*.

She paused to stir a second demerara cube into her caramel frappuccino. The iced drink had long relinquished all likeness to coffee; so much so that she no longer craved the next sip as she replaced her container on the chrome-rimmed table. Her neck muscles tensed. She glimpsed, out of the corner of her left eye, her fleece-clad supervisor, burrowing intently through the contents of an upturned paper shredder. It seemed a fruitless forage for what transpired to be little more than a dislodged pencil lead.

Here squatted an ageless figure, his aversion to stubble, coupled with a dark yet receding hairline, placing him anywhere between forty and sixty. For as long as she could recall, Zolotov had sported green-tinted spectacles: a rimless, titanium-sidepieced variant of reading glasses, narrow to the point of absurdity. Were they the clue to a rare pathological disorder? A madcap fashion statement? An underhand attempt at contrast enhancement? Alert as always to every nuance of emotion in her supervisor, she perished all hope of finding out.

Speaking as if in crying need of a nasal decongestant, Zolotov's supercilious lilt was legendary among his students; a philosophical 'think you not?' in the Russian cadences of his Oxonian swagger. The scholar would take apparent delight in hardening consonants wherever the English language permitted. Words as dissimilar as 'breadth', 'twelfth' and 'itched' all elicited the same jarring stridor, worthy to her mind of a slush machine in her native land.

Yet he remained riddled with contradictions. Just as she believed she had the measure of her supervisor, Zolotov would spring a surprise: a loathing of something she'd thought him partial to; a morbid interest in the entirely unforeseen.

One example stuck with her. Even at his most charitable, Zolotov saw imitation not as the sincerest form of flattery, but the crudest face of sycophancy. Hero worship, allied to the 'fanatical proclivities of the crowd', jostled for space on his growing hit list. Both were branded 'precursors to extremism ... thanks but no thanks ... *tochka*!' But when it came to international football, this dictum was conveniently snubbed. Zolotov would revel in the 'comforting anonymity of the *hoi polloi*' on his trips to Moscow's deafening cauldron: the Lúzhniki Stadion. Here stood the lone aficionado, replica scarf waved in patriotic zeal, obscenities hurled at the nearest of four officials whenever a slick 'one-two' was thwarted. At the tootle of the final whistle, he would be approached by a ragbag of fellow pitchsiders. More often than not, their goodwill extended to buying this intriguing character a stiff drink at Krisis Zhanra, Pokrovka Street. But the same response greeted any ill-fated attempt at conversation.

'You do *what*?'

'I teach history at Oxford.'

'You're having a laugh.'

'No, I'm deadly serious. I'm a REES professor at Oxford.'

'A what?'

'A REES professor. Russian and East European Studies.'

'Oxford, Mississippi?'

'No, Oxford University, England. Not New England. Just England.'

'You lecture students?'

'Naturally. But the whole place is leaking, no?'

'Leaking?'

'Yes, leaking. The freshmen bring so little in, the seniors take so much out.'

'Yuri! Yevgeni! Listen to this: says he stands on a podium and lectures people! By the bollocks of St Seraphim this guy is having a laugh.'

'Look . . . if you *still* don't believe me, why not pay a visit to www.clappertoncollege.com? You'll find me on the staff list.'

'Hah! Nice one, Prof. Have another *Kubanskaya*.'

*

Figueroa was jolted out of her reverie by an insistent buzz: the bell. Without looking up, Zolotov rose to his unspectacular height. He left the lounge and padded along the corridor in a fit of choler. Was it that inept postman with yet another oversize package, too cumbersome for the foyer's stacked letterboxes? Eager to view his self-made lecture 'vodcasts' in all their glory, Zolotov had taken the courageous step of ordering a VDU with the lowest achievable response time. This could well be it. Video podcasts were something only a sprinkling of faculty staff could showcase. The longer it remained that way, the better.

Squinting through his peephole, he unbolted the door for the second time in as many hours.

'Morning,' grunted a hirsute figure, copper beard trimmed to a tuft on a protruding chin. 'I came on the off-chance, namely to relieve you of the burden of my chequebook.'

'*More* impedimenta?' chuckled the Russian. 'Should find it on the dining-room table.'

Detective Chief Inspector Dárdai veered between surly and sullen. While the second-generation Hungarian prided himself on traits that inclined him to the demands of investigation, Zolotov surmised that the reverse was truer: work had been the impetus for change. The longer Dárdai remained at the Kidlington nerve centre, the more he became a prisoner of protocol, fettered by hours of plodding routine, calls for procedure and that greatest *bête noire* of all: paperwork. Like the proverbial leech, it sapped the lifeblood of creativity. Yet in his wife's devoted eyes, he was *more* than capable of matching Zolotov's feats of inspired conjecture. Frazzle the leech, and genius would resurface as swiftly as it had deserted him.

Agleam with sweat, Dárdai followed his host down the corridor and into the flat's sun-drenched belly.

'Let me introduce you to Dr. Figueroa,' enthused Zolotov after a weighty silence.

'How d'you do?' mustered the Magyar, shaking her hand coyly. The collar of his sleeveless jacket was spotted with dandruff. 'You may call me János.'

'DCI Dárdai was an acquaintance of mine at Clapperton,'

illuminated Zolotov, his voice laced with irony. 'His third-class honours degree led inexorably to a black-epauletted role in the Thames Valley Police Force, no? He has since moiled and toiled his way up the constabular ladder. From the turn of the millennium, we've collaborated on scores of highly sensitive cases. Dárdai required a personage who was soaked in the prevailing ethos of the University. His eyes and ears. A Covert Human Intelligence Source. I humbly, humbly being the operative word, obliged. A fair summary?'

'Quite,' uttered the other tonelessly. 'From the curious case of the missing Sheldonian ticket officer, who has since been found, to the chain theft of ceremonial cutlery from Clapperton which, if I recall correctly, was never quite . . .'

'Only because I had the grave misfortune to sustain an osteochondral fracture of my left femural condyle,' reeled off Zolotov, 'slap bang in the middle of interrogating Dr. Annabelle Kirkbride, our esteemed Dean. The trail went cold at the crucial moment, remember?'

'How could I *possibly* forget?' sniggered Dárdai. 'Why not regale us with the whole anecdote for the benefit of Dr. Figueroa.'

Zolotov dropped his voice by a few dozen decibels. 'This, Dárdai, is neither the time, nor the place.'

The DCI moved fast, well before Zolotov's irritation could escalate into rampant ire. 'Intriguing attempt at art,' he observed dryly, staring at the framed reproduction of Barnett Newman's *The Name I*. Overlooking the electric feature fire, it amounted to four red bands set against a variegated blue background. 'Certainly pushes artistic licence to new extremes.'

'Quite true,' returned Zolotov with renewed affability. 'Came at the twilight of Newman's artistic career. In his wake, years of fashioning that much-craved figleaf of respectability. What would *you* say the four lines signify?'

'Newman's four steps to madness: eccentricity, oddity, stupor, psychosis.'

'Frightfully droll, Chief Inspector. This masterpiece, one might say, marked Newman's decisive move from a picture to a painting, by which I mean an indivisible whole representing nothing but itself.'

Over the tops of his glasses, Zolotov gazed affectionately at what he'd come to regard as a paragon in avant-garde. It was proving to be a fascinating talking point.

'You know, I'm almost inclined to go down the Hilton Kramer route, that *New York Times* art critic who coined the phrase: "the more minimal the art, the more maximal the explanation."'

'What is there to explain?' squeezed a pokerfaced Dárdai.

'You'll notice,' drawled the other, 'that this 'zip', as Newman would later call his motif of a vertical band, is not zippy as such. It is thick and irregular, made in a series of strokes. To Newman, this strip symbolised Chaos before creation; the image that destroys the void.' He snapped his fingers. 'In contrast to Newman's later works, the blue background here is flecked and atmospheric.'

'Or is it five bands of blue obscuring a *red* background?' probed Figueroa in her broad porteño accent.

'Could well be,' conceded Zolotov, detecting coffee on her normally minted breath. 'Nothing is cast-iron at the vanguard of abstraction. But let us assume, for the sake of argument, that *The Name I* depicts four red zips. Taking into account the artist's own roots, is it unreasonable to contend that the vertical strips signify the Semitic myths of creation? Those traditions that present God and Man as a single beam of light? Remember, Rena, that the forename 'Adam' – notice how I sidestep the term 'Christian name' – is etymologically related to two other Hebrew words: 'Adom', meaning red, and 'dam', meaning blood. So the artistic rapport between red and blue,' he added with an air of resolution, 'might well symbolise Man's intimacy with the sea, sky or Chelski F.C, think you not?'

Dárdai puffed out his cheeks. 'You're introducing complexity where it is quite unwarranted.'

'Perhaps. But before we get carried away with the zip motif, there's something I've been meaning to ask you. It concerns an *Oxford Times* article I've just finished perusing.'

Dárdai smiled knowingly, eyes sloping like those of a coyote. 'I think I can guess.'

With the aid of a paperclip, Zolotov scratched the tiny pustule at the base of his chin. 'Naturally I could endeavour to guess what *you're* attempting to guess, but if my guess should be wide of the mark, or indeed should yours, I suspect we'll be back to simple guesswork.' Slowly, charily, he broke out into a wry grin. 'Perhaps for the benefit of Dr. Figueroa, who can merely hazard a guess about what we attempt to second-guess, I guess it's best if I read the article aloud, no?'

Dárdai clapped a palm to his forehead in self-ridicule. The sudden movement drew a flinch from Figueroa, her profile momentarily beclouded by a tangle of russet hair. Apparently oblivious, Zolotov trotted over to his computer desk. With a theatrical clearance of the throat, he began to read:

'A respected medical researcher faces charges of gross professional negligence.

Dr. Lomana Olembé, BA., BM., BCh (Oxon)., D.Phil (Oxon)., FRCPath, had been conducting a long-term virotherapy trial on the premises of the Churchill Hospital, Headington, Oxford. The study involved a single end-stage trialist, with fifty healthy volunteers soon to follow. Having been discharged by Olembé (Lorenex Biotherapeutics, Cheltenham), Delia J. Holdenby, 40, was pronounced dead in the early hours of Sunday, 4th of April.

Mrs. Holdenby had been suffering from an inoperable tumour. The secondary school English teacher had opted for virotherapy, an experimental cancer treatment which harnesses the oncolytic properties of viruses to target tumours that have spread to other organs. Lorenex's lead product candidate — LX-427 — is derived from a Vaccinia virus strain uniquely suited to attacking cancers.

"It is genetically modified by deleting the gene that codes for thymidine kinase", said an unnamed spokesperson for Lorenex.

"Without this enzyme, the virus cannot replicate. But human cells produce the enzyme when they are dividing, allowing the virus to thrive in metastasising cancer cells. This enhances cancer-selectivity."

Internal sources indicate that Olembé discharged Mrs. Holdenby just 48 hours after injecting the modified virus. Following heated questioning at his home, Olembé was arrested on a charge of obstructing police inquiry. He has since been bailed until further notice. A court hearing has been scheduled pending investigation.

Earlier today, a spokesperson for the Medicines and Healthcare products Regulatory Agency confirmed that Lorenex's anticipated fifty-person trial would be suspended with immediate effect. Professor Elaine Leadbitter, Director of the Inspection and Standards Division, said: "Underpinning all our work lie robust and fact-based judgements to ensure that the benefits to patients justify the risks. We believe that proceeding with the Lorenex trial would represent a dereliction of duty to a sizeable number of healthy volunteers."

The case mirrors that of Professor G. Inman (Yantonville Bio, Kansas), who faced charges of medical malpractice back in April 2009. This followed the death of 19-year-old cancer patient, Joe Tucker. The two parties were unable to reach an early negotiated settlement, and so the case proceeded to trial. Despite appealing the court's verdict, the defendant was found to be in breach of medical duty. Yantonville Bio were ordered to pay further punitive damages for conducting the human trials without the permission of the US medical authorities. The recent Lorenex trial was, by contrast, fully authorised by the MHRA.'

'Old hat,' submitted Dárdai after a brief interlude. 'Today is Tuesday, the 6th of April. Six full days have elapsed since . . .'

'Since the clinical trial, *yes*,' stole in Zolotov, 'but not the death. You're the insider. Dare I ask who supervised Olembé's questioning?'

'*I* did. My case. My trainset.'

Zolotov rolled his brown eyes with brio. 'Then don't let me disrupt your merriment. Your position, however, is not one I covet. Not one smidgen.' He sighed, puckering his brow in contemplation. 'Perhaps it calls for one of those '*Yagodka po yagodke, budet kuzovok*' heuristics, think you not?'

'What the fuck?' spluttered Dárdai.

'Berry by berry, a basket will be full', flaunted Figueroa, stifling a yawn. 'A rough rendering.'

But Dárdai was all at sea. 'Berries? Baskets? This case is all but wrapped up.'

Zolotov peered longingly at the glass-fronted liqueur cabinet cloistered away in its very own alcove. Only recently had it been restocked with *Medovukha* mead.

'You may of course be right,' he conceded, 'though I wish to delve a little deeper. Every so often, mathematicians intuit the truth of a theorem long before they are able to prove it, no? So too I sense a generous dusting of intrigue. Brace yourself for a Russian doll: a surprise within a surprise.'

'Good for you!' blasted Dárdai. 'But you'll be eating your words come May.'

Zolotov looked witheringly at the Hungarian. 'Gladly. Since when has word-eating resulted in indigestion?'

CHAPTER FOUR

'"Life would be infinitely easier if more people discarded the straitjacket of deference to the printed word, no?"'

After a three day interlude, Friday the 9th was bright and crisp. Ideal weather, thought Zolotov, to soak up the sedate charms of Bishop's Cleeve. A rare sunrise session on Google Maps UK had shown the village to be marooned in Cheltenham's sprawling outskirts. Lodged between the limestone vertebrae of the Cotswold spine, it lay at the heart of his inquiry.

At Eynsham Roundabout, he took the third exit towards a predictably forlorn B4449.

'Rachmaninoff's Third?' offered Figueroa, retracting the car window with a single tap.

'Hardly,' gnarled the Russian, covering his blind spot. 'Scriabin's one and only. F sharp minor, opus twenty!'

Entranced by the piano's sonority, Figueroa notched up the volume. 'First movement cadenza, huh?'

'That's tautological. Cadenzas never appear in anything *but* the first movement.'

'Sometimes yes, sometimes no.'

'Your point being . . .'

'That Scriabin's Piano Concerto has two quasi cadenzas: one in the first movement, one in the last.'

Humbled, Zolotov shrugged his shoulders. But he resisted the temptation of a crisp rejoinder.

Flecks of light danced off the silver Porsche. With its roof panels in place, the outside world seemed curiously remote. Hardtop detached, and its 5.7 litre V10 engine would howl like some crazed bionic banshee, assertive nose imbibing the air with wanton relish. His roadster had been landed in a Luton Airport raffle, the product of an uncharacteristic flutter en route to a winter conference at Novosibirsk State University. Included in the prize was a twelve-thousand-pound contribution towards first year insurance.

Beyond that lay only uncertainty.

Having secured sole ownership of Flat 17B by buying out his wife, Anastasiya, Zolotov had assumed the full burden of the outstanding mortgage. Before long, his professorial salary would be stretched to breaking point, quite irrespective of how many articles of outworn PC hardware he sold on eBay. He would be required to relinquish his white elephant; in favour of what, he dare not conceive. But until the arrival of that apocalyptic day, nothing would stand in the way of deep, unalloyed pleasure.

Figueroa spotted the village centrepiece from half a mile away. St Michael's & All Angels was resoundingly Norman despite a number of later embellishments. Square-towered, its narthex was screened by yawning elms extending no further than the first illegible headstones. A discordant jangling now issued from the restored turrets as Zolotov veered right into Priory Lane. Eleven o'clock. Beyond a clutch of oolite stone cottages, he pulled up by a bus stop. Lowering his car window, he caught the attention of an elderly woman in a turquoise beret. Baffled by the design of the flip-down seats, she'd installed herself atop a nearby bollard, *The Gloucestershire Echo* in hand.

'Olembé the researcher?' she ruminated, frosty blue eyes scanning the horizon. 'Ah yes. You want that nice big Georgian house opposite Sycamore Farm. Not six-hundred yards from Cleeve Hill.'

Bending his middle, ring and fifth fingers at the second knuckle, Zolotov gave his bemused subject a full Scout salute. Thoroughly pleased with himself, he restarted his engine and pulled away from the kerb. He glimpsed Cleeve Hill beyond a disused quarry, then a house that fitted the description. Of Sycamore Farm there was no sign.

Olembé's mansion was partly sheltered from the road by an *Acer campestre* in early bud. A gaunt, skeletal plexus only a week ago, the field maple was now a verdant parasol. Seeing the wrought-iron gates alluringly open, Zolotov kept his foot on the gas and drove up the path. Having parked beside a well-clipped squirrel topiary, he glanced mechanically at No. 13: entablatured doors; pediments with trefoiled tracery; twelve-paned sash windows on the first floor. He stood beside Figueroa in the portico's shade, expectant yet still, surrounded by a quartet of sun-bleached pillars. The Argentine wore a mauve satin blouse and white hip-huggers. Zolotov was dressed for adversity: a single-breasted pinstriped suit with tapered sides. His collar plainly struggled to accommodate his broad Windsor knot. Not that it mattered. Flattening his slick, dark hair in a single sweep, he reached for the brass knocker beneath the filigree fanlight.

Within seconds, the great door was unbolted. Dishevelled, unshaven and sporting creased Bermuda shorts, Olembé eyed them mistrustfully through his silver-rimmed shades. But before he could relieve the tension on his pursed lips, Zolotov had launched into a stylised monologue.

'The name's Zolotov. Heard about the whole shebang via a sprinkling of intimate sources.' He laughed gratingly. 'Oh yes, I know what you're thinking, Doctor. There they stand, not-so-clandestine journalists, with nothing better to do than to . . .'

'But even if you *are*,' interjected Olembé, 'I've no objection to you hearing my side of the story. But only on one condition.'

Zolotov squashed the gnat that had been pestering him since their arrival, but resumed his attention immediately.

'Do not prejudge. Picture yourselves in my position, however onerous the task.' He heaved a sigh of distress. 'Local tongues just keep on wagging; and if the media continue with their same old scaremongering tricks, local news will become national news. National news, international. I know this much: I'm damned if I'm cleared, finished if I'm charged.'

'Can't comment on the last part,' confessed Zolotov, 'but you're dead right about the media. Life would be *infinitely* easier if more people discarded the straitjacket of deference to the printed word, no?'

Bereft of patience, the Cameroonian chuckled tepidly in agreement. He led them into a spacious entrance hall, floor furnished with oriental rugs. A staircase scaled the middle of the hallway, then peeled off to the right. The lounge décor was broadly in keeping with the Georgian façade: glass teardrop chandeliers; burgundy upholstery; shield-backed chairs.

'A rare April sunburst,' remarked Olembé prosaically, gesturing them into a rustic kitchen. Two spent cans of Red Bull stood on the countertop beside a container of Prozac, seal broken. Facing them was a blue lacquerware bowl, piled high with kumquats, papaya and overripe kiwi fruit. As if aware that the mere sight of his medication would arouse undue curiosity, the doctor placed a hand into his shirt pocket, withdrew a key, hurriedly unlocked the patio door, and politely bid them follow.

Symmetry and harmony were the keynotes of grandeur in Olembé's garden. The sloping lawn was a close-cropped sward of brilliant green, almost unnaturally so. It was bisected by a path, tangled sweet pea climbers forming a shaded walkway beneath the bamboo trelliswork.

'Hey, I love your pond!' gushed Figueroa instinctively.

Olembé gazed at the rod-shaped water feature, bordered on three sides by a rockery. Caressing its surface was a miniature cascade, first meandering through the crevices of moss-encrusted basalt, before thrusting swords of light across the water. A curtain of spray hissed its way into the spring air.

'Used to be a bio-pool,' explained the doctor, 'though maintenance has been a bit touch-and-go lately. Run-off from lawn fertiliser has made it something of an expo for eutrophication.'

Seeing the blankness in Zolotov's eyes through the veneer of an assured nod, Olembé went on to explain how the processes in his pond were a microcosm of those occurring in algae-ridden lakes.

'A glut of nutrients – frequently caused by raw sewage or agricultural run-off – triggers an overgrowth of algal blooms. These outcompete standard plants. When the plants die, their decaying matter becomes dinner for a host of microorganisms. As the bacteria proliferate, they consume the dissolved oxygen. A high percentage of aquatic life suffocates, a serious issue when people depend on the fish for subsistence. This reminds me: can I offer either of you a drink?'

Figueroa looked guiltily at her wristwatch, russet hair tousled by the breeze. 'Too early for a spritzer?'

'Oh, go right ahead!' leapt in Zolotov, giving his knee a jovial clout. 'Seeing as I'm driving, I'll have my Bloody Mary sin alcol.'

Her surprise was ill-concealed: never before had the finer points of highway law deterred Konstantin Zolotov.

Olembé disappeared into the kitchen, leaving his guests to melt into deckchairs beneath the awning. They drew in the pergola's woody aromas, the clang and clatter of wind chimes, the long churr of a glossy-billed house sparrow. Figueroa amused herself by flicking through an old copy of Private Eye, peering at the cartoons, disregarding the speech bubbles. As Zolotov brooded over whether to lend his host a hand, Olembé emerged from the kitchen, mirrorshades stationed at the ridge of his hairless scalp. With bewildering gallantry, he wheeled in an oval side-table, metal handles cut into the deep redwood gallery. A tingle of unease passed through the Russian. Why had Olembé gone to such extreme lengths for a pair of unsolicited strangers? What had possessed this eminent scientist in the throes of trauma, professional and personal?

'So what does your wife make of all this?'

Receiving her spritzer, Figueroa had couched the question as delicately as she could muster. She soon regretted her impulse.

'I . . . I lost her three years ago,' faltered Olembé, shutting his eyes in desolation. 'Three years almost to the day. Mballa died of a rare lung disorder called idiopathic pulmonary fibrosis. Specialists at the JR gave her two years. She surpassed that estimate by four months. You see . . . compared to, say, cystic fibrosis, the cause of IPF is practically unknown in medical spheres, or as Asimov once put it, "idiopathic is nothing but a high-flown term to conceal ignorance". The experience left me, a medic, feeling utterly ineffectual. Mballa was barely forty-one.'

So what of his ineffectuality? To Zolotov, the facts were not in question – Olembé's wife had almost certainly lived, ailed, died, and in so doing, left her widower with an implacable sense of powerlessness. Rather, it was the impact on Olembé's psyche, more specifically his *id*, that fascinated Zolotov. In that dark repository of instinctual desires, was there not an urge to remedy the injustice? To expedite emotional closure? Coordinating the virotherapy trials might have stemmed from a desire to offer hope to the downhearted; hope so cruelly denied to Mballa. That was the benign explanation. Or had Mballa's death filled Olembé with an almost clinical need to reclaim control? To shape the fates of patients under his care – women no older than his own dead wife?

'From that day onwards,' continued Olembé, 'my lips have been pressed against life's bitter cup. Seems like only yesterday that Mballa took silk. Saw to it that she was buried in her ceremonial QC vestments: silk gown, long-sleeved waistcoat, horsehair wig, black breeches, black stockings, black rosette. All the colours of mourning. Why do I mention this? For no other reason than to illustrate the scope of her achievements. A first-class mind. So unfulfilled.' He looked up at the stone parapet obscuring the slate roof. 'Mballa was the chief breadwinner in our household. Kept us afloat. Without her, the future of this wondrous building is shrouded in doubt.' He tailed off, eyes resting on the rim of Figueroa's glass. 'And now *this*,' he supplied, shaking his head in incredulity.

The physical change had been profound. Olembé's lids now drooped heavily over his eyes, the once outstretched legs crossed protectively over one another, as if he were seeking refuge from the cold gust of reality. When he next spoke, he did so in an oddly toneless voice; suppressed shame, perhaps, for betraying such an unmanly spectrum of emotion. A lack of self-restraint.

'*The Oxford Times* have made me out to be some soulless, self-serving, pathologically deluded crusader. Think what you will about the last two, but I simply *won't* have them saying I'm soulless. How can you accuse me of being case-hardened when Delia was my one and only human trialist?' He exhaled deeply. 'Of course I'm moved by what happened. Why shouldn't I be? But the fact remains: if Mballa were alive today, and in Delia's position, I would've followed the same script.' He squeezed his temples with the tips of his fingers. 'While I wouldn't go so far as to say that Delia had *nothing* to lose – no true Catholic would! – she had, statistically speaking, rather less to lose than a patient with a more localised and uncomplicated tumour. Spontaneous remission? Out of the question. Much as I hate relegating the human race to a functional commodity, I felt it justified the audacious attempt. Like it or not,' he continued, regaining control of his features, 'there's a quantum leap between animal and human models. Put simply, the molecular microenvironment in a rodent cannot adequately reflect the conditions inside a person. Take the innate immune system, for instance. Its activity in humans is controlled by the Vitamin D Receptor. In mice, it rests on the shoulders of that grand signalling molecule, nitric oxide. The result? Considerable variation in how each species fights disease; discrepancies so large, that even the most sophisticated molecular modelling software fails to correct for them. Hence our need for human trials.'

He repositioned his mirrorshades with a nimble flick of the thumb.

'Hardly surprising when you consider that humans and mice diverged seventy million years ago.'

'Yes, indeed,' remarked Zolotov without irony. 'Intriguing creatures, think you not?'

'Humans?'

'Mice, Doctor. Mice. If only more of us could learn to live with our heads a half-inch off the ground.'

Olembé smiled wearily. 'Can't disagree there.'

'Wouldn't expect you to, Doctor. Speaking of which, did you ever give Delia a chance to disagree?'

Olembé seemed unmoved by the bluntness of the question. 'She was well aware of the risks, if that's what you mean. For an experiment to be ethical, researchers must obtain informed consent from the human subject.' He dropped his voice to a husky whisper. 'I don't play mind-games with my trialists. I tell them like it is.'

'But why are you telling *us* this, Doctor?'

'I'll answer that with a question of my own: what do I gain from honouring patient confidentiality? Zilch. Tried it a few days ago and got arrested for obstruction. Having paid my bail money, I managed to convince DCI Dárdai – don't get me started on him! – that I wouldn't abscond, or endanger the public whilst on bail, or interfere with witnesses. After the trial,' he mouthed affectedly, 'whose verdict is essentially a foregone conclusion, I'll have a token twenty-eight days to appeal. Then, God only knows.'

Figueroa peered searchingly at the haunted face, pleading for empathy, or at least some measure of understanding. One more impropriety would turn him to dust. Warily, she uttered: 'People in your profession are usually covered by indemnity insurance, right?'

'So what if they *are*?' jerked out Olembé, resettling his glass with a thud. 'Just think of the negative publicity this business has already washed ashore. Spiteful, scathing publicity!' His voice fell as sharply as it had risen. 'In my profession, reputation is everything. It is the master key to the myriad locks of research funding. As a private company, Lorenex relies heavily on the support of a small but dedicated band of investors. Lose them, and all R&D operations crumble overnight. We then have our sundry charitable foundations,' he supplied with distaste. 'The ficklest people imaginable. And don't forget the revenue from co-marketing and co-promoting new products. Partnerships, in other words. Since February, we've had a nominal licensing arrangement with a Kobe-based firm. Once our trials proceed to phase three, our partners will have the exclusive right to manufacture *Vaccinia* LX-427 for the Japanese market. They, in return, will pay us a royalty on all commercial sales.'

Zolotov stabbed at his highball glass with a plastic stirrer. 'So recent events won't make for happy reading.'

'Too right they won't! Lose these corporate alliances, and Lorenex can only nosedive.' His kinaesthetic rendering of a stricken dive bomber was most convincing. 'As if *that* was not enough, Delia's death has left our Executive Chairman in the lurch.'

Zolotov's pulse quickened. 'Lurch, Doctor?' But his mind was racing ahead of his words.

'Allow me to deconstruct the issue. Only last month, Professor Trent received a rather unexpected offer for his controlling stake in Lorenex. It came from Brett Milligan, head honcho and founder of BramTech, Sellicks Beach, South Australia. Says a lot about the guy when the name of his electronics firm is an acronym of his initials. A bit like Amstrad and Sir Alan. But I'm drifting. Professor Trent had been hoping to bow out on a high. Sixty-seven in August. When I mobiled him before the trial, he made it crystal clear that he stood to pocket a hefty profit once the buyout went through. Somewhere around the seven million mark, in fact. This Milligan guy claims to have a special interest in pharmaceuticals and is . . .'

'Just another asset-stripper!' appended Figueroa with a jingle of her silver bangles.

'I hardly think so,' said the doctor tetchily. 'Which isn't to say he's some tender alms-giver: profit is profit. But until the morning of Delia's death, Milligan had promised not only to clear our debts, but to relocate the business to Southwark's hip new waterfront in time for the London Olympics. Brilliant for company prestige, you'll agree, and a guaranteed hike in earnings for us all. Needless to say, his interest has frozen solid. So keen is Milligan to distance himself from virotherapy at large, that he's approached a

Vancouver-based firm specialising in monoclonal antibodies. And no prizes for guessing whom Trent blames for our Aussie's U-turn.' He threw his guests a sidelong glance. 'Like it or not, this isn't a simple case of *res ipsa loquitur*.'

'Ah, the thing speaks for itself,' showboated Zolotov, toasting the doctor with his empty glass. 'A legal concept, important in medical malpractice cases, whereby technical incompetence can be inferred from the mere fact that an injury occurred, no?'

'Impressive. Do I detect a medical degree?'

'Merely an eight-month taster, Doctor. Opted to follow in my father's contrails – a pratfall in itself – and soon found the unholy trinity of blood, formaldehyde and cadaveric leers a little too . . . well . . . Shelleyan.' He stuck out an arm as if to redirect the tides of discourse. 'You were saying.'

'Now where were we? Ah yes: *res ipsa loquitur*. You must've heard that oft-quoted tale about the patient who consults his GP over shooting pains in his abdomen just weeks after a routine appendix removal. The GP arranges for an X-ray, the upshot of which is that there's a metal object the size and shape of a scalpel burrowed in the patient's large intestine. That, you'll agree, is an open-and-shut case because the facts are so transparent. The plaintiff need hardly break sweat. My case is different.'

Zolotov waited for Olembé to elaborate. What he expected was a cold, clinical evaluation of why the doctor had deemed Delia fit to leave hospital after only two days; or how far his criteria for what constituted a stable condition tallied with those of his scientific peers; or what a hypothetically perfect trial might have achieved; or what judicial benchmarks were used in selecting expert witnesses. What he got was a frenzied effusion.

'I should be cloned, not chastised! How can I possibly help the dying when I'm off the GMC register, for crying out loud? Negligence is what her oncologist should be answering for! The negligence of defeatism and inaction. *His* is the gutless credo of . . .'

'Look!' rejoined Zolotov, wiping a dot of sweat from his thin upper lip. 'This isn't about the principle but the after-care, no? You must, as I see it, sway the jury by substantiating one of the following claims. One,' he said airily, holding up an index finger. 'Delia died from a cancer-related shutdown, entirely independent of the virotherapy injection you administered. The normal-course-of-events argument. Two: Delia died *neither* of cancer, *nor* in response to virotherapy, but from a secondary affliction due to her compromised state of immunity. One she developed whilst in the care of her oncology specialist. Which went unnoticed by staff at the John Radcliffe. Either way, your decision to discharge her within forty-eight hours would no longer constitute laxity on your part. The prosecution might see it differently, of course.'

Something in the glibness of his manner, the hollowness of his stare, told Figueroa that Zolotov was gracing familiar ground.

Olembé raised a quizzical eyebrow, weighing his options. 'Your second hypothesis being somewhat less plausible,' he submitted at last, 'I think I'll content myself with the first.'

Zolotov craned his neck skywards, his self-righteous gaze unmistakable code for 'as you wish.' His words were murmured. '*Kon' o chetyryokh nogakh, da i tot spotykaetsya.*'

The Cameroonian recoiled. 'Say again.'

'A horse has four legs, but continues to stumble,' clarified Figueroa, pleased to get in on the act. 'My colleague is intimating that even the most competent people can, and do, make mistakes. To be construed, I would assume, as an elaborate form of self-reproof by Mr. Zolotov. A self-flagellatory . . .'

But Olembé would have none of it. 'Oh *do* spill the beans. Which of us three is the horse?'

Zolotov slid lackadaisically to the edge of his deckchair. 'I'm sure you'll agree, Doctor, that we all, to varying extents, exhibit equine behaviour in our more deluded moments, no? The peripheral vision that discerns the tangentially positioned predator, but is blind to what lies ahead. Put another way,' he continued, 'some things are better seen at a distance than at close proximity. I too was guilty of this in my more impressionable years,' he reassured the nonplussed Olembé, 'if you see what I'm driving at?'

'Naturally,' avowed Figueroa, somewhat unconvincingly.

Olembé offered a wavering smile. 'Perhaps I will when you stop speaking Martian. Incidentally, shouldn't you have been taking all this down?'

'If I *were* who you think I am, then I suppose I might have done so,' deadpanned Zolotov.

'Yes, but who do you think *I* think you are?'

'Say again.'

'You heard me.'

'I think *you* think we're undercover columnists,' to which Olembé nodded spiritedly, 'but I can assure you, Doctor, that this is not the case. In the meantime, I wish you a calm and fruitful afternoon.'

And over forty miles away, in the adjacent county, Delia Holdenby lay supine in a basement mortuary, putrefying piecemeal.

*

Despite Zolotov's appeals to forgo lunch altogether, they dined at an unedifying Bishop's Cleeve café. Not so much a café, thought the Russian, as a provincial greasy spoon. The tabletop looked grimy, the wood ringed with dried lard. Few items on the menu departed from that illustrious troika of 'English Breakfast', 'Olympic Breakfast' and 'Jumbo Olympic Breakfast', a two-pound increment at each milestone. It soon transpired that the first and third specialities differed only in the volume of baked beans splattered over two bacon rashers, lovelessly frazzled to the texture of garnet sandpaper. Spaghetti hoops, soused in a mucilaginous mess masquerading as tomato sauce, swamped both plates. Experience alone should have alerted Zolotov to the likely repercussions, for by the time he'd re-entered his Porsche, he was chewing on his third Rennie peppermint.

Ordinarily, the REES Professor might have wallowed a while longer in the waters of self-pity.

But not today.

Certainly not today.

CHAPTER FIVE

"'If and when you hit the dizzying heights of professorship, you'll learn that dissimulation is the law of the jungle.'"

The Porsche purred forward, coasting through undulating woodland, accelerating boldly into the hairpins. Burford Golf Club sprawled ahead to the right. Beyond its tree-lined fairways lay fields of oilseed rape – a yellow cloth, textured by knotting and hitching motifs, hedgerow borders tapering like excess yarn along the fringes of hand-loomed fabric.

Three tawny hares bounded across the road. With a flash of scuts and a flurry of leaves, they found the sanctuary of brushwood with seconds to spare. But their brinksmanship was lost on the suit-clad Russian. One hand cupped the steering wheel; the other gripped the ash gearknob until white crescents appeared on his knuckles. The apparent dearth of gravity gave him the impression of being suspended, rather than nestled, in his bucket seat.

And still Figueroa sat upright, every limb in her body tightly knotted. She kept checking the rear-view mirror as if convinced that they were being followed. Undeterred,

Zolotov broke the silence with the phlegmatic air of a beer loafer. 'A penny for your thoughts?'

'You don't wanna hear them,' she retorted in a tone that dissuaded further exchange.

He heaved a thoughtful sigh. 'Is that likely, Rena?'

'Look. I'm uncomfortable with the whole Holdenby thing, okay.'

'Which part?'

'Your plan to show up unannounced at his house.' Disconcerted by her supervisor's cascade of shrugs, she spoke with heightened intensity. 'My mother always taught me to respect grief as something sensitive; something personal. What makes you think you can just override my sense of right and wrong?'

'You think I'm thick-skinned?'

She answered him with a waspish waggle of the head.

'Fantastic.'

'What's fantastic?'

'Your riotous naivety. You forget that thick skin is as much a virtue as a vice.'

'Please explain.'

Zolotov gave her a broad, if overweening, smile. 'I call it Drysuit Theory. You may not be aware that neoprene drysuits, like the one Dárdai wore in the Baltic last spring, contain millions of tiny air bubbles.'

'Dárdai actually wore one?'

'More than once. I call it life! The air bubbles form a waterproof shell with the sole purpose of insulating our grateful wearer. Great for diving beneath ice sheets. If, however, we notch up the water temperature, this 'thick skin' suddenly becomes burdensome. Our overheated user pines for a thinner, looser, open-cell garment. He must adapt to his milieu. And fast.'

'The model sophist! So adroit, but so unsound!'

'And why would *that* be, *dorogaya moya*?'

'Because if our Holdenby visit threatens to plunge us into legalistic hot water, it follows that we require a thinner skin. A wetsuit, not a drysuit. Sensitivity.'

'That would depend on how scalding our hot water is, Rena. In the meantime, why not spare me the psychobabble and refrain from investing your words with the slushy authority of an American TV diet guru. Is that too much to ask?'

It evidently was. Stung by his high-handedness, Figueroa pouted her lips by way of a reply.

But her colleague's enthusiasm knew no bounds. 'Late on Wednesday, I googled 'Holdenby + Oxford + Headington'. You'll be pleased to know that Richard Quentin Holdenby is, to all intents and purposes, one of us.'

'How d'you mean?'

'I mean he knows his diphthong from his diaeresis, no? Transpires he's a ghostwriter for a bevy of local personalities: soap starlet Janine Seimes, virtuoso oboist Douglas Broadwood, Sir Bernard Holstein OBE, Joel Austin, the Premier League fooballer. The common link? A disinclination, or indeed inability, to do their own writing.'

'Impressive,' mumbled Figueroa, chewing seductively on her spearmint gum. 'Tell me more.'

Zolotov leaned in as close as his seatbelt would allow. 'He, being Holdenby, specialised in painstakingly researched obituaries for the weekly edition of *Varsity*, the older of the two Cambridge student papers. Barely twenty-five when he was appointed Deputy Tory Party researcher in the run-up to the 1992 General Election.' He sighed wistfully. 'And therein lies a sliver of disparity between Holdenby and myself, no? English being his mother tongue, Holdenby enjoyed something of a head start in lofty circles. Though privileged to spend my formative years with the embattled *Chronicle of Current Events* in Leningrad, it wasn't until the age of twenty-nine – yes, twenty-nine! – that I became editor of the Clapperton student monthly. No special treatment. Just another mature student, and a foreign one at that.' He gave his red gemstone a birdlike peck. 'So what if I'd powered against the Brezhnevian tide? So what if I'd risked everything to circumvent those apparatchiks at the State Committee for Publishing? At Oxford, my past counted for nothing. No-*thing*!'

'Simply fascinating,' scoffed Figueroa, her porteño accent broader than ever. 'But why do you tell me this?'

Zolotov waved her away. 'Ex-dissident or not, I'll always be a du—'

'A Jew?'

'—tiful citizen.'

'Oh, I thought you meant . . .'

'Hah! Got you again. This side of the Baltic, I'll always

be a dutiful citizen. Am I prepared to don the garb of the vigilante? *Net.* Do I carry a search warrant? *Net.* Would I dream of forging one? *Ni za chto!* You see, Rena, I rely on goodwill or outright stupidity to gain access. As both are out of my control, I turn to . . .'

'Gain access?' protested Figueroa, throwing a sanctimonious glance in the direction of Charterville Allotments. 'I much prefer the word 'admittance'. Access sounds so crude. So KGB.'

'Funny you should say that. Do me a favour and open the glovebox.'

Spreading her fingers in mock strangulation, Figueroa did as she was asked. Having felt around for the nearest object to hand, she extracted a pack of aquamarine business cards. The logo seemed vaguely familiar: an italicised 'A' immured by 2D tubes. Each card was stylishly finished with silver edging.

'Had these printed yesterday,' rhapsodised the Russian. 'For the next hour, Rena, I am not Konstantin Zolotov, but Roman Rinatovich Kolotov, Chief Executive Officer of ARENSEFT Marketing and Trading. A man entrusted with company expansion in line with ARENSEFT's global gas strategy. Liquefied natural gas, that is. The proud recipient of an MSc in Theoretical Physics from Oxford University and a PhD in Nuclear Physics from the Kurchatov Institute of Atomic Energy in Moscow. A thirty percent shareholder of the relatively obscure FC Krylya Sovetov Samara, perennial underachievers in the Russian Premier League.'

'Yes, but will *Holdenby* have heard of the firm?'

'Certainly. It's a UK-registered subsidiary of Russia's largest gas producer. A Trojan horse into the lucrative British gas market.'

'And me?'

'ARENSEFT Solutions Architect perhaps. Haven't quite decided.'

'You mean I'm going incognito as *well*?'

'But of course.'

'Why?'

'Affectation and pretence, Rena – the blueprint for success. He, that is to say Holdenby, will presume I'm some hard-boiled gas mogul; one of those oligarchs who capitalised on the economic chaos of the perestroika years by amassing a great, if questionable, fortune; whose abiding influence in energy, telecommunications and metallurgy was secured by Yeltsin's loans for shares scheme of 1995-6.' His right eyelid twitched. 'Holdenby will be under the distinct impression that he is being commissioned to ghostwrite an autobiography: *my* story, on *my* terms, money no object. A lay bare account. A debunking of myths. A product so saleable, he'd be a fool to turn me down.'

Figueroa shot him her most corrosive look to date. 'But that's deceitful! The whole plan is an abuse of trust!'

'Not at all. I need to speak to Holdenby. For that, I require a pretext. This is it.' His fingers drummed the dashboard. 'If and when you hit the dizzying heights of professorship, you'll learn that dissimulation is the law of the jungle.'

'¡Dios mío!' she spluttered, cheeks flushed with colour. 'There I was thinking that honesty is always the best policy.'

Zolotov notched up the air-conditioning with an urgency belying his unflurried exterior. 'Have you ever paused to consider the demands on a departmental streamliner like myself? I am required to shape the contours of our academic vehicle so as to ensure optimal resistance to the fluid of impending dissolution, or worse still, amalgamation. All this, whilst complying with the draconian University guidelines on the departmental quota of research associates.' He discharged a half-suppressed laugh. 'Has it ever occurred to you just how I managed to keep Leszek Witkowski, that narcissistic nitwit, at arm's length from our department? How I foiled his proposed secondment from Non-Russian Slavonic Studies despite his grasp of Early Cyrillic being infinitely more secure than your own?'

Figueroa's resistance was beginning to crumble. 'Look, I really didn't mean to . . .'

'And if *I* were Holdenby,' Zolotov interjected tautly, 'I'd sooner collaborate with such a character than place obstacles in their path. I'd show them in, offer a glass or two of Jerez Dulce, listen to their proposal, and accept their unrevised manuscript. I'd avoid probing too deep and for too long.'

'Er, hello?' heckled Figueroa. 'Someone's living in cuckoo land!'

'And one more thing,' snapped Zolotov, disregarding

an amber traffic light. 'I've e-booked a ticket at the Oxford Playhouse tonight. Seven-thirty sharp.'

'Why, what's on?'

'Pirandello's *Sei personaggi in cerca d'autore*, or for your benefit, Six Characters in Search of an Author. Having gorged myself on the tart pomace of meta-theatre, I plan on sampling the piquant, chilli-emboldened jungle curry peculiar to Chiang Mai Kitchen. As things stand, I shall be dining there alone.'

'What about me?'

'You?' returned Zolotov, mimicking her accent to a tee. 'Go to the nearest solarium, and top up your tan!'

*

By quarter past four, Zolotov had parked outside *The White Horse* in Headington. Beaming at his roadster with proprietary pride, he locked its doors via a crested key fob. The car drew envious stares from a posse of hooded youths, diverted from refining stepovers with a football. But as Figueroa emerged from the cockpit, russet hair combing her satin blouse, their interest in the Porsche began to flutter.

No. 2 had a warm, prosperous exterior, enhanced by newly repointed brickwork and elaborate lamps flanking the porch. A Sky Digital mini-dish protruded from the chimney, evidence of the area's lenient conservation laws. A maroon Audi R8 stood in the driveway. Beyond an adjoining gate lay a well-proportioned garden, its single flowerbed awash with scarlet begonia and ultramarine bellflowers. Beneath some

Pampas grass, face turned away from his new arrivals, crouched a man with a ruffled thatch of auburn hair. Zolotov noticed that an infrared device was strapped to his left wrist. He appeared to be pointing it at a mounted sprinkler outlet. So far, to little avail.

Hearing the crunch of displaced gravel, the man swung round defensively. 'Yes! What is it you want?' he spat, thickset arms poking out of his pullover. While his hazel eyes were neither red-rimmed, nor bloodshot, sickle-shaped discolorations beneath the lower lids bore witness to intense distress. Distress and exhaustion.

'It's rather important, *actually*.' Zolotov rolled his head ever so slightly in the direction of the stationary Audi. 'We were hoping to speak to a certain Mr. Holdenby.'

'Speaking!' retorted the ghostwriter after a protracted lull. His expression was stuck between a jeer and a challenge, a contemptuous curl to the mouth and bulging eyes lending him an irresistibly amphibian appearance. 'Roe-MAN Ko-LOH-toff?' he faltered, receiving a pristine business card with grubby hands. 'Don't tell me you're the latest nuclear disarmament contributor to *The Morning Star*.'

Zolotov held up a warning finger, more in flippancy than in menace. 'Two consecutive UK Business Secretaries have attempted to call me that! Here, watch my mouth move: **RO**-man **KO**-lo-tov.'

But Holdenby was barely listening. His disparaging eyes flitted between the card and the broad ring-binder tucked under Zolotov's shoulder. Gradually, his face began to lighten.

'Wait here,' he said at last, simultaneously chaining the porch door from the inside. 'I'll be back shortly.'

Standing by their second doorstep of the day, Figueroa gave her supervisor a waggish jab in the ribs. 'A spanner in the works, Professor?'

Zolotov reset his glasses on the bridge of his aquiline nose. 'Not at all. What I neglected to tell you is that Roman Kolotov is real.'

'Real like Vladimir Putin, or real like the Chupacabra?'

Zolotov hadn't heard of the Central American cryptid, and so decided to skirt the question. 'A couple of days ago, Rena, I entered 'Roman Kolotov' into Wikipedia's famous search box ... as Holdenby is surely doing now. He won't be disappointed – my business card tallies with the article on every level. Before I collected you from Clapperton this morning, I uploaded a recent photograph of myself in place of our CEO's authenticating headshot. Remember, Rena: any old buttinsky can edit.' He smiled crookedly. 'How long it remains there before the *real* Roman Kolotov replaces it with his own is anybody's guess.'

The ghostwriter duly returned, moving more freely than before. When he next spoke, it was as if an invisible thread of tension had slackened.

'You'd better come in,' he purled, trying to sound placatory. He led them over the threshold and into the porch. Halfway down the corridor, they turned into an L-shaped room: a buff-carpeted lounge. Zolotov cast his eyes about furtively. Bright and spacious, the colour palette was too overtly pink for his liking. He did, however, see the value in a glass-domed conservatory even if cloudless afternoons represented the exception rather than the rule.

A plasma TV presided over the far wall, volume muted, picture animate. Across it flashed a replay of Samir Nasri's dazzling slalom from the previous month's Champions League clash with Porto. Arsenal's reward for sharp-witted interplay had come against a Portuguese outfit managed by the imperturbable Jesualdo Ferreira. Rankled by the away team's craven reliance on long-ball tactics, Zolotov had watched no further than the seventieth minute. Not that he had an emotional stake in the outcome.

Scattered across the dining table were several items of correspondence – some torn asunder without the aid of a letter knife, others still sealed. A metallic device resembling a giant tabletop stapler stood against the wall. Beside it, a digital organ console. But it was Holdenby's chess set that enthralled Zolotov the most. Carved from an unidentifiable wood – though instinct told him it was ebony – each blemishless piece was fitted with a black leather base. No felt in sight. He imagined the board as having deep, satin-lined hollows; 'trays' in the jargon of the cognoscente.

'Was trying my hand at the Scholar's Mate,' explained the ghostwriter. 'Pitting myself against my own wits. I call the white pieces 'Holdenby 1', the black ones 'Holdenby 2'. You'll notice that the white queen and bishop are joining forces in an attack on f7 and . . .'

'Easily neutralised by moving your black pawn to g6,' inserted Zolotov, 'elegantly countering the white queen's move to h5'. He picked up a black rook and held it knowingly to his nose. 'Fine-grained ebony heartwood, no?' he hazarded. 'The real McCoy, if that is the correct idiom?'

'Just about. I take it you're impressed?'

'Quite unreservedly. I covet the object without envying the owner. Speaking of which, do you recall that documentary exploring claims of cheating by IBM?' He scratched his head oafishly, catching the incredulous eye of his research associate. 'Whatever did they call it?'

"Game Over: Kasparov and the Machine," said Holdenby, sounding more constipated than smug. 'It claimed that Deep Blue's well-publicised victory was nothing more than an elaborate IBM artifice to pep up its stock value. Kasparov spoke of a deep, almost human, creativity in the machine's moves. Exasperated when IBM retired Deep Blue without a rematch.'

'Indeed he was. But I'm sure you'll agree, Mr. Holdenby, that there is nothing – absolutely nothing! – that isn't *bona fide* about the FIDE itself. *Bona fide* FIDE, in fact.'

'Fédération Internationale des Échecs,' reeled off Figueroa.

'Yes, I know, I *know*,' said Holdenby in his impetuous way. 'And might I add, Molotov, or whatever your name is, that the parroting of timeworn quips fails to elicit tears of . . .'

'Not at all,' scythed through Zolotov, smoothing his hair with his wrist. 'The joke was impromptu, I can assure you.'

'Look!' blasted the other. 'I can't believe you've come

here to talk about chess! And why do you insist on standing when I've twice gestured you to sit?'

As they finally took their allotted seats, Holdenby peered at Figueroa as if for the very first time. 'Who's this?' His question might have sounded offensive were it not for the falsetto of genuine curiosity.

'Do forgive me. This is my handpicked associate, Doctor Catalina Duarte de la Peña.' The Argentine covered her flinch with a flutter of mauve-tipped eyelashes.

'So why are you here?' demanded Holdenby, calmly disregarding Figueroa.

Zolotov answered him in a soft drone. 'I'm a busy man, Mr. Holdenby, but not too busy to notice your name on the flyleaf of the recent Bernard Holstein autobiography.' Inching forward guardedly, he handed over the ring-binder. 'My preliminary manuscript: the bad, the very bad, and the downright ugly. What you see before you is clumsy and disjointed, extracts from diary entries, newspaper cuttings and so on. I turn to you, a seasoned ghost, for assistance.' He rolled his eyes. 'A friend of mine suggested 'Confessions of an Oligarch' as the working title. I, however, have always warmed to 'Blackwash: Roman Kolotov Tells All'. My advice? Skim it later, or you'll never put it down.'

Mouth agape, Holdenby tilted back as far as the recliner would allow. His earlier aloofness, his smouldering impatience, had all but gone.

Zolotov struck while the iron was hot. 'May we express our deepest sympathies for your loss, Mr. Holdenby. We heard about it in the news.'

The widower sharpened his stare. 'Still haven't quite internalised it all,' he heaved, struggling to bridle the tremor in his voice. 'The whole thing began with this peculiar sensation behind her breastbone, as if the food itself was silently burning its way through her gullet. Hot or cold; light or stodgy; gloppy or crispy – not a jot of difference. At first, we put it down to a nasty case of indigestion; and it wouldn't have been the first time those problem kids at school had cranked up her bile. Just to be on the safe side, I took Delia to see our GP. Nice guy, very experienced, known him for years. He palpated her chest a bit, shone a little blue light down her throat, and told her to cut out coffee and cabbage. Fast forward two months, and we found ourselves reading, then rereading, the results of her barium meal. Even before the Greek bloke had authorised an endoscopy, he was talking about palliative measures and the importance of positive thinking. My mother-in-law summed things up when she suggested, point-blank, that I send Delia to that "nice little hospice in Leopold Street". That was dementia speaking. Of course Delia and I would have none of it. After the diagnosis, I effectively turned night into day. Online research. Hours of it. My clients' autobiographies could wait – assuming, of course, that they remained my clients. Then this Olembé guy shakes his gory locks and everyone, Delia included, is given fresh hope. Can't think why I'm telling you all this.'

Zolotov fine-tuned the position of his glasses. 'Grief does peculiar things to us, Mr. Holdenby. I for one should know.

But why the sizzling cynicism? Any underlying reasons you wish to share with us?'

'What a perfectly crass question! Behind every cynic lies a disenchanted idealist. That's me in a nutshell. Nothing I say or do can bring Delia back, but stopping that incompetent quack in his tracks would be the closest thing to a consolation.' Encountering only silence, he turned to them in anguished appeal. '*Do* try and put yourselves in my position. Wouldn't you, in respectful memory of your wife, sister, brother, do the very same?'

Zolotov smiled inadvisably. 'So you consider him culpable of a major misjudgement?'

'That's the general idea. Our biggest issue, and I think I speak for the whole family, is with the length of hospitalisation. Forty-eight hours always seemed so offhand, so arbitrary. I may not be an expert, but I know this much: a two-day quarantine doesn't allow anywhere *near* enough time to rule out all possible complications. Why not longer? Lorenex cost-cutting, pure and simple.'

'Forgive me, but what exactly do you mean?'

'During our consultation at Savinaud Place, Olembé assured me that Delia would be reimbursed for the 'inconvenience' of being a trialist. Indeed she was – her cheque arrived this morning. Six hundred pounds deducted from the Lorenex coffers,' he added, his voice thick with irony. 'Don't tell me that a longer quarantine would've bled the company dry. You know, it's almost as if they wanted Delia off their backs in time for the next trial.'

'The healthy volunteer study?'

'The very same. That, apparently, is higher up the clinico-corporate ladder.'

'So it would seem. But tell us, Mr. Holdenby: when your wife returned to London Road, was it to an empty house?'

'More or less. But visitors were more than welcome.'

'Visitors?'

'Delia's Lutheran pastor, for instance; the usual clutch of well-meaning parishioners; oh, and some Jock called Philomena – a lifetime member of the Oxford University Chess Club. My bedside manner isn't the best, so I covered all bases by hiring a professional nurse. Olembé's orders. In her heart of hearts, Delia knew that her needs would mount before they diminished. And there was never any guarantee that they *would* diminish. Eager that I be "protected", as she put it, she consented to the idea of a helper.'

'So how did she measure up? This nurse, I mean.'

'Was just getting there,' bristled Holdenby, flicking off the plasma TV. 'Scatty and highly strung, if you must know. Redford was her name. Yes, she enjoyed talking up the dignity of the bedridden, but still managed to arrive fifteen minutes late. Twice.' He continued amid snivels of emotion. 'When the paramedics failed in their attempts to . . . to resuscitate Delia, that po-faced bitch has the impudence to tell me – lecture me! – on how my wife was naïve to approach Dr. Olembé. A heresy of sentiment! Did that Redford woman *honestly* expect Delia to lie down and yield to the cancer? To accept our joint fates as the mere peaks and troughs of life?'

'Was she from an agency?'

'A part-time health visitor working under the stewardship of the Nursing and Midwifery Council. The NMC is a nationwide regulator that keeps tabs on the quality of practice and so on. Anyway, to cut a long story short, Redford advertised herself in the *Oxford Journal*. She, if I recall correctly, did six years geriatric nursing at the Radcliffe Infirmary. Could have been more, only the Infirmary closed for medical use in 2007. In happier economic times, Redford might've relocated to purpose-built buildings at the JR and continued where she left off. Clearly she was seeking pastures new.'

'I see,' intoned Zolotov, as graciously as he could muster. 'Seeing as my colleague and I don't wish to intrude any further . . . oh! – and about the manuscript.'

'*Nil desperandum*,' said Holdenby. 'Rest assured that I'll give your opus a quick once-over. A summary judgement, if you like. I need to familiarise myself with the subject matter before we can start discussing structure. Once I get your voice on tape, I'll do all I can to capture your innermost thoughts, fears, partialities; to tell your story in the most faithful and compelling way possible. I'd ask that you make a cheque payable to RH Ltd at each fifty-page milestone. Leave me your email address, and I'll get back to you with comments.'

'Email address?' rebounded Zolotov, suddenly unnerved. 'Isn't it on the card I gave you?'

Holdenby shook his auburn mane, studying both sides. 'Better write it down.'

Zolotov fumbled around in his innumerable pockets. The

ghostwriter grasped his predicament and offered a ballpoint. On the back of the business card, Zolotov scribbled kolotov@arenseft.co.uk. He made a show of asking Figueroa whether she thought his squiggles legible, tutted at his own ineptitude, and placed the card on a nearby side-table. As Holdenby began to rise, the Russian held up a rawboned hand.

'Do not vex yourself, my friend. We'll see ourselves out.'

*

Zolotov angled his car sedately out of the tight parking slot – sedately, for he remained blissfully unaware of the left wing mirror's proximity to a stationary Piaggio MP3.

'Helpful, wasn't he?' presented Figueroa, grudgingly accepting a dollop of sanitising gel from her colleague. 'Seemed to mellow a bit towards the end, huh?'

'Hmmmm . . . certainly helpful on the autobiographical front. Shame it wasn't our *real* reason for visiting.'

'Tell me honestly: what *was* in that ring-binder you gave him?'

'Ni'aha!' chortled Zolotov, fastening his seatbelt belatedly. 'Seeing as the idea only came to me recently, I opted for the path of least resistance, no? Booted up, googled 'Project Gutenberg', pinned down the e-version of *The Kerensky Memoirs: Russia and History's Turning Point (1967)* – the best I could do in the circumstances – selected fast draft on Print Properties, and ran off the entire book. Three kilograms of it, all on premium paper. Though I scrupulously omitted two details.'

'Oh?'

'Title page and preface, Rena. Would have given the game away rather sooner than one might have liked.'

PART TWO

CHAPTER SIX

'Scarcely had she uttered this most prosaic of questions when her voice assumed an uncharacteristic brittleness, blue-veined hands brushing the sides of her grey twill cardigan.'

Unusually for a Saturday evening, Imogen Redford poured herself a glass of water – Aqua-Pura, a slice of lime, nothing else. After the excesses of Thursday night, she was on a self-imposed detox until her guests arrived.

With her heavy-rimmed glasses, drab mustard hair and fondness for sexless sweaters, Redford was neither 'hip', nor 'bling', nor 'happening'. She came to regard clubbing as a means to a social end; a shield from the mundanities of suburban existence. Sandwiched between Oxford Ice Rink and Oxpens Service Station, Coven II had fast become one of her favourite haunts. When empty, it had the aura of a disused warehouse: black walls, corrugated ceiling, no windows or trimmings. When teeming with revellers, the basement metamorphosed into an illusory realm of timelessness, pounding breakbeats and visual distortion creating a deep, if fleeting, sense of camaraderie. Then phase two: a shared spliff in an exit stairwell; surreptitious thigh contact in that throbbing arena of seduction; a clinical act of coition in a blue-lit cubicle. Coldly impersonal, but thrilling nonetheless.

Now thirty-two, Redford had been a PPE undergraduate at Tresingham College, Oxford. A Dr. Carol Peterson progress report, written at the close of Michaelmas 1996, went like so:

> *'Not always the sharpest falx foenaria on the farm, yet admirable in her determination to rewrite the rules of Heraclitean dialectic. Nuance passes her by. The sooner she develops an intuitive understanding of the difference between 'a priori' and 'a posteriori' knowledge the better. Like the true intellectual saprophyte, Imogen derives her conceptual nourishment from dead or decaying matter, contributing little in the way of original wisdom. Never have I dealt with one so rampant in their raillery, deftly exploiting every caesura to force an entrance. Lengthways, widthways and edgeways have long been the interpolative hallmarks of an 'Imogen' tutorial.'*

Never quick to become envenomed by ridicule, Redford had taken the appraisal in her stride. Academically she was still a greenhorn, a tenderfoot, a tyro. If she left Oxford without embarking on a doctorate, so be it. A career in academia was electrifying, but better left in the hands of naturals.

Fate intervened at a critical juncture.

Three days before she was due to sit her first Finals paper at the High Street Examination Schools, Redford contracted glandular fever. Cooped up in her charmless cell of a bedroom on staircase IV, the girl's lymph nodes had quadrupled in size. The doctor at the Jericho Health Centre had prescribed the usual: ample rest, a course of painkillers and not a drop of alcohol. Fortunately for Redford, Tresingham had confirmed its self-styled reputation as 'the friendly college' by championing her claim for special consideration. Satisfied that she'd met all the requirements of the degree programme – and that macheting her way through eight examination thickets was beyond sanity – the University had awarded an aegrotat. This classless degree gave her the benefit of any lingering doubts over her credentials: it assumed that perfect health would have produced a pass. No more, no less.

Invariably approachable, Redford had attempted to forge friendships. Two tutors had entered her circle of trust.

The first, a certain Dr. Philomena Rae, taught Applied Econometrics at Tresingham College. Like so many in her profession, the pink-faced SNP partisan was never one to suffer 'bampots' gladly; 'numpties', if she found herself in the company of friends. Despite the generational disparity, it was Rae's jaunty air and complete lack of pretension that endeared her to Redford; a capacity for self-mockery largely absent in Redford's peers. Their extracurricular bonds were forged by their shared membership of the Tresingham Borodin Orchestra. Unrepentantly selective, the ensemble subjected its prospective members to two rounds of auditioning before a prudish panel – one, if their instrument was as high in demand as Redford's contrabassoon. The recompense came in the form of subsidised tours across

Europe. The alabaster cliffs of Møns Klint, the red and white arches of Córdoba's Mezquita, and the wood-sculpted figures adorning the Mariacki altarpiece in Kraków, had all – at one point or another – thrust their way onto the TBO schedule. Philomena Rae had been as ever-present as her piccolo.

The second, Professor Dame Olsten, was an accomplished amateur violinist. With her upswept crown of hoary hair and pronounced overbite, Judith Olsten drew strength from her reputation as a fair, if fearsome, don. She lived alone, loved alone, and had no intention of departing her world anything other than a spinster. None but a clutch of fellow musicians had witnessed Redford's vigorous CPR as her tutor lay unconscious at the foot of Basilique du Sacré-Cœur, Montmartre. That was back in August, 1997. On learning that their newest patient had defied the odds by surviving a 'thrombus-induced heart attack', doctors at the Salpêtrière had conveyed their astonishment in fractured English. Fresh from a four-day first aid course, Redford had snatched life from the snares of certain death.

Olsten would remain beholden to her former tutee, not only for her timely intervention, but for the daily visits while she recuperated in a packed, cheerless ward. The Enlightenment Ontology Professor had reciprocated the goodwill by offering to assist Redford in all future ventures. As if to underline her gratitude, the Dame had promised to 'flush out any bugbears that may disembogue into your sea of tranquillity, my dear'.

She would remain true to her word.

Within months of graduating, Redford became the relieved tenant of a semi-detached 1950s house in Abingdon-on-Thames, a market-town some seven miles downstream of the City of Oxford. Her 'two rooms up, two rooms down' affair on Cotman Close soon became earmarked for gentrification. Gone would be the leaking radiators, the friable asbestos insulation, the vinyl-framed windows, the vagarious attic boiler. Polished wooden floors would supplant her corn-yellow rugs. The wall partitioning the lounge and kitchenette would be knocked through to create a versatile, open-plan entertainment area. With revaluation, the Band E property (£88,001 to £120,000) would soar to a Band G (£160,001 to £320,000).

But there was a catch.

In anticipation of the commensurate increase in council tax, Redford's landlord had doubled her monthly rent. The new amount was strictly non-negotiable. Her arrears mushroomed. With her father deceased and her estranged mother now a naturalised New Zealander, two obvious routes to salvation were shut. After five months of coercive letters and threats of eviction, her contract was officially declared void by Oxford Magistrates Court. Reluctant to be dispossessed in favour of an upwardly mobile young couple, Redford had tested the sincerity of Olsten's offer. The Dame had duly obliged, bankrolling the outstanding sum with interest, and ensuring that her former tutee was granted an immediate relief from forfeiture.

Half the promised upgrades failed to materialise. But as far as Olsten was concerned, that was entirely beside the point.

*

Having vacuumed every corner of the lounge, and added four drops of bergamot oil to her spirit burner, Redford had jogged down to the local delicatessen to replenish her dwindling supply of rollmops. Poppy seed bread, she judged, would counterbalance the pickled herrings most competently. Her main course owed much to a 2009 issue of *Sainsbury's Magazine*. Feather steak casserole would be served in a deep Römertopf. The clay cooking pot would rest on a steel hotplate. Before the eyes of her guests, its contents would be spooned into three colcannon hollows, each seasoned with ground green pepper and a dusting of cinnamon. There would be no offer of seconds.

'Feather steak?' warbled Philomena Rae, receiving her heaped plateful. 'How noble of you.'

'Hope you like it,' returned Redford, not taking the bait. 'And you'll be pleased to know that my ankle fracture is no more. The doctor gave me the all-clear about ten days ago. You know, I actually broke out into a run on my way to the Polish deli. Should be playing badminton at Iffley Road in no time!'

'Smashing,' said Olsten without irony. 'Now that we've got *that* particular monkey off our backs, there's something I've been meaning to discuss; something that's been playing on my already fraught mind.'

'Oh?' probed Rae, running a stubby finger through her clump of jet-black hair.

'The Olembé business. You must have seen it in the papers. I first met Delia at one of our more memorable Bach Vespers. A bright, agreeable, articulate girl, quite without the vitiating literal-mindedness of so many St Columba's parishioners. I heard about her cancer trial relatively late on – we weren't *that* close, you understand. A few days before she was due to leave for the Churchill, I decided to drop in on her. Seemed in reasonably fine fettle. Danish pastries aside, I brought along one of those effusive "my thoughts are with you even though you and I both know that you're a goner" cards. Couldn't arrive empty-handed, now, could I?' The Dame turned to an intrigued Rae. 'Did *you* read the article, Philomena?'

'Aye,' affirmed the Glaswegian. 'I paid a visit on the day Delia was discharged from the trial centre. Came to offer moral support and an obliging ear. Little did I know then that her condition would deteriorate with such grim rapidity.'

'How well did you know her?' grilled the irrepressible Olsten, subjecting Rae to a toothy smile.

'We were members of the OUCCS: the Oxford University Chess Club Seniors. Delia was a real thorn in my side, bless her. Beat me to the Best Player Award following our gallant loss in last year's varsity match. Only last month, Delia stunned everyone by playing a table-topping match for the OUCCS 1sts. A Tuesday evening. How she struggled down to Tresingham in her condition is quite beyond me.'

Redford tittered girlishly. 'I might consider joining some

day. Does the OUCCS field teams for the county league as well?'

'Yes, we contribute four,' said Rae hurriedly. 'But you're in danger of missing the point. From a dying woman's perspective, continued attendance required an iron will. Superhuman resolve. The least we can do is acknowledge her quiet courage.'

'Hadn't thought of it like that,' confessed Redford. 'But isn't it awful how researchers are allowed to endanger patients for the sake of some piffling medical knowledge? Knowledge that may or may not benefit science in the future? People who condone this are on the verge of a very slippery slope.'

'Ho hum,' sighed Dame Olsten. 'The news coverage has given us to understand that Delia 'reacted' to whatever that Olembé chap administered.' She melted into a conspiratorial smile. 'Suppose someone from a rival R&D firm infiltrated the trial in a bid to discredit Lorenex. Sabotage. Foul play. Why not, I ask you both?'

'Always possible,' conceded Redford, blue eyes fixed on the watery remains of her casserole, 'but hardly likely. The threat of crippling penalties, lawsuits and scandal would surely deter them.'

'Would it?' persisted Olsten, dabbing her lips with a paper napkin. 'Not sure I follow.'

'It's painfully simple, Judith. Even if your hypothetical conspirators evaded detection, sabotaging a rival's first human trial would be pure, unadulterated suicide.' She met Olsten's defiant gaze. 'I hope you'll agree that the more discredited the concept of virotherapy, the less attractive the saboteurs' *own* company to investors. A blatant case of shitting on your own doorstep.'

But Olsten was unimpressed. 'You allow minutiae to befog the bigger picture, Imogen. The question *I'm* posing, merely as a devil's advocate, is whether any measures were taken to rule out the possibility of foul play? I daresay a post-mortem would straighten out this whole sorry affair. It might even confirm my second pet theory.' Rae and Redford lowered their wineglasses in flawless synchronicity. 'That in his efforts to test the power of psychosomatic recovery, Olembé administered nothing more than a pla . . . pla . . .'

'A placebo?' offered Redford.

'Bravo, Imogen. Got it in one! The old brain isn't what it was, eh?' Eager to maintain her earlier momentum, Olsten changed tack. 'Oh, and you won't believe who I saw in Debenhams this afternoon: George Fawkins, arch-scoundrel incarnate!'

Redford was unusually pensive. 'You apply the term "incarnate" to an atheist? Charming. I'm pleased to say I've just finished reading *God: A wishful mirage.*'

'And?' squeezed Rae.

'And I see sense in his claim that God's existence should be treated with as much scepticism as any scientific hypothesis.' She broke off to stifle a sneeze. 'If all goes well, his book might finally muffle the theological bugle, not to mention that trite riposte: "oh, it's purely a matter of Faith."' She looked at Rae imploringly. 'Why oh why can't more people wake up and smell the coffee of pragmatism and logic?'

Olsten's furrowed face twisted into a sneer. 'How very quaint. You speak of logic and pragmatism all too liberally, as if stale watchwords are enough to substantiate your contention. Far from it, my dear.'

'How diplomatic of you,' returned Redford, exploiting the assertive browlines of her spectacles. 'You've spoken for a full twenty seconds and said almost nothing.'

'Then you'll feel right at home. Do not think me brusque, Imogen, but you shouldn't allow your infatuation with Fawkins to blind you to his own hypocrisy.'

'My *what*?' gasped Redford, now the colour of a boiled crayfish.

'Let me put it to you this way,' hissed Olsten. 'All the tentativeness, regulations and meticulous research that underlie scholarly science – the very criteria that Fawkins would be swift not only to advocate, but to adopt – fade away spectacularly when that atheistic bigot attempts to reduce the irreducible . . . much like a student submitting an essay on Kant without ever having read the *Critique of Pure Reason*. In many ways, Fawkins is as much a confessor of faith as I, an evangelical Lutheran, might call myself.'

'You mean that zealous faith exists in the purest science?'

'Glad you've finally seen the light, Imogen.'

'But I never said I agreed!' retorted Redford. 'How can you accuse evolutionary biologists of blind faith when the theory of natural selection is supported by a whole corpus of evidence? Contrast this with creationist dogma, backed by some ancient scrawl.'

'The point I intended to convey, my dear, was that for all their apparent polarity, religion and science converge when you consider the assumptions under which they operate.'

'How?'

'First things first, Imogen. With religion, our unprovable component needs no introduction: belief in a superhuman creator; obedience to a personal God or gods as the source of salvation.'

'And science?' harassed Redford.

'With science, Imogen, our position is somewhat subtler. Here, our difficulties stem from a compulsive *need* to prove.' The Dame paused to lick her lips in exhilaration. 'Notice how scientists are lured into the trap of assuming that the world's origins are rational; that our universe's physical phenomena must, by their mere existence, be explicable via the two E's: experience and experiment. Need I elaborate, Imogen?'

'The suspense devours us.'

Olsten drew a hand across her flaccid neck in a cut-throat gesture. 'That was cheap, Imogen, or "schlock" in the parlance of our Master, Reuben Gershman. No matter. If what I say sounds strangely familiar, it might be that you're subconsciously recalling chapter three of my recent book.'

'Haven't read it,' countered Redford. 'Doing so would require bribery on your part and drunkenness on mine.'

Rae expelled a hoot of approval. Then, witnessing

Olsten's affronted grimace, she stopped herself in her yet shallow tracks.

'What's woeful,' resumed Redford, 'is your stiff-necked conviction that religion should be impervious to scientific scrutiny. Tell me straight: why *shouldn't* the God Question be tackled like any other?'

'Like any other what?'

'Any other hypothesis in science.'

'I'll tell you why not!' rejoined Olsten spiritedly. 'Because for a hypothesis to be called scientific, it must be able to be tested in conformity with scientifically recognised methods.'

Redford nodded, albeit jadedly.

'But to subject the God Question to scientific scrutiny would be the height of cretinism. Put differently, Imogen, how can one even *attempt* to schematise something like faith, when faith, almost by definition, entails belief in a truth that cannot be proven? Yes, modern science can elucidate the auditory mechanisms of the human ear, yet it struggles to explain why the lush harmonies of a Borodin symphony succeed in stirring our souls. Or why some souls are more easily stirred than others.'

Redford winced irreverently. 'If current science can't answer such questions, perhaps future science *will*. But religion, current or future, doesn't have a hope in hell!'

'An unfortunate choice of words, Imogen. Do not misunderstand me,' she appended, just as Redford prepared to flex her tongue. 'As a body of techniques for gathering observable, measurable and replicatable evidence, the scientific method is largely invaluable. You'll surely remind me that without advances in medicine, I'd already be checking into the wooden Waldorf.'

'She'd be dead,' clarified the Scot, as if for Redford's sole benefit.

'Thanks for that, Philomena. But you'll agree that to grasp the limitations of science is as key to intellectual nourishment as bridling the fanaticism of the faithful. Look no further than the Middle Way.'

'Broadly speaking,' twittered Rae, 'I'm inclined to agree.' She made a shapeless beast of her fingers. 'While I can only cringe at the religious ring-fencing of so many evangelicals, I'd say Judith's line is *infinitely* more moderate. Aye, certain concepts are unfit to be placed beneath the distorting glass of outside scrutiny.'

'As Freud was doing when he turned his undeniable talents to an analysis of miracles,' supplied the Dame. 'Like so many of his contemporaries, poor old Sigmund was hindered by his reluctance to explore religion on its own terms; at its own level of experience.' She folded her napkin in a gesture of finality. 'Would either of you care for a coffee?'

Scarcely had she uttered this most prosaic of questions when her voice assumed an uncharacteristic brittleness, blue-veined hands brushing the sides of her grey twill cardigan.

'Life's been so . . . shall we say . . . roily at my end recently, I've come to equate all menial tasks with escapism rather than tedium. A refuge of sorts.' Eyes widening, she gave a quick, restless smile. 'Imogen: you take your coffee white, if I recall correctly?'

'Yes,' said Redford crustily. 'How *very* considerate. Two sugars for me, please.'

'Just the one for me,' trilled Rae, giving her colleague a confirmatory thumbs-up.

Composure recovered, Olsten acknowledged the orders and bobbed her way to the back of the house. By virtue of previous visits to Redford's, she knew this to be the site of a squalid kitchenette. Among its fittings was a gas stove, a sink unit with a lone drainer, and a melamine worktop with PVC edging. Spartan but functional, thought Olsten as she spooned some coarse grind into a *cafetière*. Standard rental décor. Still, one can't feel guilty. It's not as if I'm her mother; and if it wasn't for me, Imogen wouldn't even have a roof over her head. At least not *this* roof.

Without waiting for Olsten to disappear from earshot, Rae turned to Redford in feigned sympathy. 'Please don't take this the wrong way, Imogen, but your earlier point on theologians requires revision. Aye, a theologian is a true Proteus: part historian, part philosopher, part philologist, and dare I say it, part scientist. I've yet to meet a theologian who mindlessly brandishes the "oh, it's purely a matter of Faith" banner. At least not a self-respecting one.'

Redford's tone was far from urbane. 'Misplaced idealism – that's what *your* problem is. My experience of theologians could hardly be more different, insofar as . . .'

'Or does your penchant for oversimplification ensure

their rhetoric falls on deaf ears?' spewed a triumphant Rae. But before Redford could deflect the slur, Olsten had shuffled back into the dining room. On her tray stood three earthenware mugs.

'So, Imogen,' she cooed, handing out the coffee-filled mugs. 'Rather than donning the militant garb of a reductionist, acknowledge the selfhood of *both* realms, scientific and religious alike. Oh, I've forgotten to bring the milk!'

'How remiss,' sniggered Redford, pouncing at this unexpected opportunity to flee the barrage. 'I'll get it myself.' With a tut of disapproval, she left in a gust of cedar and sandalwood.

Rae sipped what remained of her inky red Lambrusco. 'It's a tad out of my remit,' she mused, 'but I believe it was Gould, Stephen Jay Gould, who coined the term "Non-Overlapping Magisteria". I really cannot think of a more fitting description for the domains of religion and science.'

The Dame nodded, coupled by a sharp intake of breath. 'Couldn't agree more. While the scientific realm can be seen as a forum for empirical debate, addressing the crucial 'what', 'why' and 'why ever not' questions about our universe, the religious realm extends over questions of ultimate meaning. Moral value. Those who attempt to fuse the two, or seek to use the apparatus of one as a springboard from which to assail the other, succeed only in dampening the glory of each.'

With the flourish of a conjuror, Olsten whipped off the

tartan cloth covering her rattan hamper. 'And *do* help yourself to these chestnut purée éclairs,' she beamed, baring a sallow pair of foreteeth. 'I trust the taxi ride hasn't left them overly traumatised. My pastry. My icing.'

CHAPTER SEVEN

'He disliked the inept, almost neurotic, bobbing of the head, the unsteady eyes that quailed beneath his gaze.'

'You heard of Cardigan Street?'

'Aye laddie,' avowed the cabbie with a knowing smile. 'Hop in!'

At six-foot-three, Reverend Travis cut a commanding figure. Brick-jawed and barrel-chested, he shunned modern hairstyles in favour of a self-abnegating Caesar cut. Provided he kept his trembling hands in the pockets of his surplice, few would have believed him an alcoholic. The only clue to a weakness for spirits, the torque of dependency, came from the heat spots emblazoning both cheeks. To a stranger, they might have passed for blushing. A simple handshake banished such illusions.

Back in 2005, Travis had traded the faux-aged friezes of Yale, New Haven, for the floral cornices of Eldridge Hall. Tucked away on the Banbury Road in central North Oxford, the Permanent Private Hall reared high over a nineteenth century cricket pavilion at the heart of University Parks. Like thousands before him, the

Texan was drawn to its international reputation for excellence in theological education and ministerial formation. More in tune with his denomination than any other PPH, the Hall's forty-page prospectus had pressed home its evangelical ethos. That October, the fledgling Marshall Scholar had embarked upon an M.Phil in Theology, opting to specialise in Christian Ethics. In so doing, he'd joined a privileged list of Pulitzer Prize winners, CEOs and Supreme Court justices, all united in their readiness to consummate the special relationship. His Yuletide ordination was as much an embrace of gospel values as a rejection of secular realities – or, in the words of General G. C. Marshall himself, 'this turbulent world of today'.

The service had ended at 5.55 sharp. He was scheduled to meet an elderly parishioner in the Bill Thomson Room. For over a week, the woman in question had been meaning to speak to him about a 'private and sensitive' matter. They'd arrived at the swift conclusion that St Columba's halogen-lit committee room, equipped with two flip-chart easels, would provide ample scope for privacy. From *whom*, he could only surmise. True to form, the matter had hijacked his attention more than once throughout his inaugural sermon, manifesting itself in a series of wistful pauses and pained gazes. Unable to contain his anxiety, he'd lingered in the lobby for the Lutheran throng to disperse. With no sign of the pensioner, he'd jettisoned his white Eastertide stole, locked the vestry door, and mobiled for a 001 Taxi.

They rounded *The Bear Inn* at Alfred Street's intersection with Blue Boar Street. Four-fifths into the manoeuvre, Travis was unnerved by a sharp snap. He grasped, after a cursory scan, that it was the sound of the door pegs, activated by the central locking system. Finding this more than peculiar, he stiffened his spine in anticipation of the cabbie's next move.

The Scot poked his tiny cranium from behind the head restraint. 'Wee bit more crime than before,' he chirped, blubber lips parting to reveal a deep groove in one of his front choppers.

Travis sneezed apologetically into his right palm. 'Come again?'

'Petty crime, laddie. Petty crime. Always go for the auld cailleachs' handbags. Like sitting ducks, thay are, *specially* in these urban bottlenecks. Wouldn't try guessing what thay'd be keeping thare, mind. Toys for thair geobags, ma gash-gabbit brother says.' He smiled ruefully. 'But ye hae a fair and truthfu' office.'

Travis could best be described as tongue-tied. Swamped by a lethargy that only bourbon could induce, the banter passed him by. Not that sobriety would have made the slightest difference – the cabbie might as well have been speaking Maori. Travis retreated to safer ground.

'Not from round here, are you?'

'Not a dreepin' chance!' guffawed the other, angling

his car erratically into Hythe Bridge Street. 'Ye probably don't know that ma auld parents' lodge sits at the gateway to Galloway and the Solway Firth. Not two miles frae Devorgilla Bridge.'

'I didn't,' confessed Travis. 'You speak in riddles.'

'Thenk ye, laddie!'

'That wasn't meant to be a compliment.'

'Dinna fash yersel,' burbled the driver, breaking out into another contrite smirk. 'Still high after the *Doonhamers* turned on the style, ye see. Can smell promotion in the air! Been a Queen of the South diehard since I was a bairn.'

'Queen of the South? So I guess your family are monarchists, then.'

'God nae!' spewed the cabbie, delighting in the flatness of his vowels. 'Whatever made ye think that? Queen of the South are made to sweat for thair money. Queen Lizzie gets off scot-free!'

With that, he dissolved into paroxysms of high-pitched laughter, scarcely eluding a delivery van that had pulled up outside the Oxford University Press building.

Travis failed to see the joke. 'Soccer?' he offered at last, desperate to make amends. But as they neared the end of Walton Street, his humiliation deepened.

'Getting warmer, laddie. We call it footie in these parts.'

*

By six-twenty, Travis found himself in the heart of Jericho and its seemingly endless rows of Victorian terraces. The sky was newspaper-grey.

'Ye faan asleep, laddie? That'll be ten for the ride.'

Travis dug his heels into the rubber car mat. 'Baloney! The folks on the phone said nine.'

'In the name of the wee man!' cried the driver with a plaintive, rather than reproachful, inflection in his voice. 'What will I be tellin' the wifie . . . that on a Sawbath nicht, and a ruddy guid claik with a parson, I canna ask for a wee bit more?'

'Then there ain't no better cause,' gnarled Travis. He slammed the door and handed over a ten-pound note. On another occasion, he might have added – 'what better way to make a man's day?' – but thought better of it.

Rolling down his window, the cabbie's lips slackened. 'It's a wee bit like caustic soda, if ye ask me.'

'Come again?' The engine's splutter had failed to enlighten the nonplussed pastor.

'Money, laddie. Money. Water it down, or it burns the flesh!' But before Travis could venture a reply, the elated cabbie had given his engine a full-throttle blast, careered round the corner, and vanished.

Travis stood stock-still beside a blossoming bird cherry, a sickly almond scent emanating from its creamy-white flowers. The pavement offered scant protection from the scooters, cars and vans that rumbled past sporadically. To his right was a two-storey house with a *Finders Keepers*

'TO LET' sign. From it emerged two teenage girls, the taller one struggling to restrain a fractious Pomeranian. The blundering runt waddled along on its scarcely coordinated spriglets, a thoroughly convincing cross between a chinchilla and a scatter rug. Attached to its collar was a short-braided leash with a loop handle; the type used for obedience training. By Travis' reckoning, obedience wasn't the foremost item on the canine agenda.

A screech of skidding tyres spilled out into the street. The Lutheran was hard-pressed to understand those who burned their rubber in a fanfare of misplaced machismo. Fitting, perhaps, for the maelstrom of Miami's Little Havana, or a seedy Neapolitan backstreet. But what place had it in Jericho, a suburb deriving its name from the oldest continuously inhabited city in the world? With his abiding contempt for 'those darned godless swine', Travis would remain in perpetual search of the fabled British cult of understatement.

One by one, the streetlights began to flicker. St Barnabas' campanile loomed ahead to his left, just one of Sir Arthur Blomfield's many Romanesque brainchildren. As he trudged along the pavement in the belfry's general direction, he began to intone the brooding lines of his compatriot, T.S. Eliot:

'. . . Every street lamp that I pass
Beats like a fatalistic drum,
And through the spaces of the dark
Midnight shakes the memory
As a madman shakes a dead geranium . . .'

The parishioner in question had spoken of net curtains. She clearly hadn't planned on being visited, so there'd been no mention of a house number. Only 36 fitted the description. Its façade was more quaint than inspiring, with a lacing of whitewashed bricks treated to one too few coats of blue paint. Travis puckered his brow and pressed the bell. He held his breath.

The door opened to reveal a prepossessing countenance. High-cheekboned and oval, it tapered meekly to a slender, dignified chin. The girl's yellow tank top was deeply scooped, exposing the delicate structure of her clavicle. Yet she seemed acutely unsure of herself. Her bow had been a little too subservient. He disliked the inept, almost neurotic, bobbing of the head, the unsteady eyes that quailed beneath his gaze. He put her at nineteen, possibly twenty. Sri Lankan? Indian? The Texan wouldn't wager on either.

'Do I know you?'

The girl offered a tentative smile, a suggestion of gloss on her thin lips. 'No, sir,' she squeaked. 'I'm Melissa. I do the cleaning.'

An artery throbbed in his throat. 'But I don't understand. Where's Dame Olsten?'

She gave him a fixed, glassy grin. 'Fast asleep, innit?'

Blind to what impelled him, Travis lurched his way past the startled girl. Not stopping to reset the pine console table he'd upended, he tore up a narrow staircase. Still flustered by the strain, he pounded instinctively at the only closed door on the landing.

'You there, Judith?'

No response.

He bellowed anew.

Silence.

Swallowing hard, he placed a hand on the brass doorknob. A full ten seconds later, he pushed.

CHAPTER EIGHT

'"You know what, Inspector? You might've just hit the mark without meaning to."'

A sight to melt the sternest nerves.

A fatalistic drum.

He peered into the dark room, papered in alternating bands of magenta and beige. A wicker side-table stood by the curtained window. Stationed at its centre, as if on a rostrum, was an aluminium-capped lava lamp. Orange spheroids caromed off the bottle's sides, colliding but not cohering. His pale grey eyes were drawn to a double bed. Slumped in front of its chintz-quilted headboard, arms thrown out on either side, lay a hoary-haired figure. The upturned nose, the high-domed forehead, the protruding teeth – all wrenchingly familiar.

Other than that, she might have been a stranger. Stagnant blood had been drawn to the contours of her face. Two crusty channels beneath her septum bore witness to a recent nosebleed. Where once the eyes had shone with a vitality belying their counsel of years, they now assumed a filmy, bulbous, bovine character – unseeing, yet fixed idly on his bourbon-stained dog collar. Forceful and domineering even in death, they chided him for his sweaty dishevelment; for the gracelessness with which he'd discovered her pitiful body.

Olsten, Travis presumed, had been maliciously attacked. How else had she sustained such rampant bruising? There was something very odd about that Asian girl. He had seen it; smelt it. He pictured her, cool and calculating, biding her time as the ribcage rose and fell, primed to strike with her bare hands and smother the fragile face in a fit of deranged ferocity. Unmoved by her victim's frenzied gasps, the waning limbs that thumped the mattress like some goliath cricket.

Travis knew what had to be done. Amid snatches of fetid air, he grabbed at his mobile. Muscles benumbed by shock, he darted towards an open door at the end of the landing: Olsten's bathroom. He slammed it shut, then twisted the showerhead above the clawfoot tub. A fitful stream dashed its surface, suitably loud. He swivelled round to face the toilet. Above it hung a cistern, dangling chain connected to a flush lever. Pull it, and he would seal all cracks in his makeshift sound barrier.

Steadying both hands, Travis yanked the D-ring chain. Through the splutter, he dialled '911'. Two rings later, he realised his mistake, cancelled the call, and punched in a triple '9'.

*

Cold fists of rain pummelled the pavement with merciless vigour. The torrent formed rivulets which, after lapping the tyres of several parked cars, spiralled into the gutter. Two Vauxhall Astras slid to a halt. Riled at having been parted from his wife's goulash, DCI Dárdai gave the passenger door a cavalier thrust until its hinges squealed. Stepping out, he eluded two oil-streaked puddles, before spattering his socks with the sludge of an unnoticed third.

Dárdai's sergeant, some ten years his junior, sought shelter from the windswept street. Clearing both nostrils, he scoured the sky in exasperation. *'Fuck my boots! Bloody fucking April! Bring on the fucking summer!'* To run down the clock, he would wait inside the warm car and tune-in to 102.6 MHz. Who knows? He might even catch a few snippets of Hit 40 UK before being called away to take statements. Tedious, brain-numbing statements.

Dárdai turned towards his Scene of Crime Officers. 'Gregson! Brown! You cover the main entrance. Douala! Carpenter! Cordon off the area and man the back gate, capiche?'

Finding the front door invitingly ajar, he entered the dingy hallway with practised authority. Tailing him was Dr. Russell Popham, sprucely attired in a disposable white overall and gloves. As Dárdai jammed the rubber doorstop into position, he was accosted by the pervasive odour of feline urine. Then a tinkling bell. Still leading the way, he traced its source to the adjoining room. Galled by this barefaced show of evasion, he reached for his warrant card and placed a brawny hand on the doorknob.

Dárdai was not a shining beacon when it came to local history. Far from it. He relied, instead, on an ever-deepening pool of anecdotes, most of them amassed during interviews with elderly Jerichonians.

Back in the 1950s, the suburb had been stippled with bordellos and massage parlours. Through each paper-thin wall, one session of horizontal callisthenics soon became melodically entwined with the moans of adjacent liaisons. One particular prude had called it 'an aperture, or rather an orifice, for post-war sleaze'. Plans to replace the area with light industry and new housing had met with mass disapproval. Years would elapse before this drastic redevelopment programme was tempered to an acceptable level. Irreparable houses were demolished, others modernised at the dawn of the Me Decade with the aid of council grants. Pivoting his neck about the hall, Dárdai was intrigued as to how No. 36 had escaped these mandatory upgrades. He put it down to a quirk of history. Nothing more.

The sitting room was frayed and forlorn. A bowl of potpourri stood by the blackened hearth. Beside its limestone mantelpiece, ensconced in a red wing chair, sat a fetching young lady. A tattoo crept out of one of her skin-tight leggings, an amulet that receded gradually as it neared the mid calf. Her attention seemed to be consumed by the amber-eyed cat that rubbed itself ingratiatingly against her waxed shins. From the moggy's docility, Dárdai presumed the ritual was familiar to both parties.

A tall man looked on dazedly. His ankle-length vestments betrayed his holy office; a denomination Dárdai struggled to place. In the moments before the man had registered Dárdai's arrival, he'd been pacing to and fro in his leather roper boots, muttering inaudibly, the hems of his white robes billowing like wings in the wind. But his troubled expression had vanished on demand.

'Inspector!' gushed Travis, as Dr. Popham sidled in behind Dárdai. 'I was gettin' *mighty* . . .'

'Never mind that,' barked the DCI. 'Show me the body.'

'Sorry, Inspector. She's upstairs.'

Without another word, the unlikely quartet filed out of the lounge and up the stairs. They paused at the threshold to Olsten's bedroom. Slipping on a fresh pair of polythene overshoes, Popham approached the double bed. In stolid silence, he went through the formality of checking for a pulse. Dárdai preferred to linger – he cruised the tiny room, cracking his knuckles with customary abandon.

'Who found the body?'

'I did,' replied Travis. 'But I guess I wasn't the first.'

'What brought you here?' pumped Dárdai, disregarding the insubordinate flavour of the retort. 'Drawn by extrasensory perception, were you?'

'You know what, Inspector? You might've just hit the mark without meaning to. I had an appointment with

Judith at six o'clock tonight; at St Columba's, our Church. When she didn't show, I just . . .'

'Showed up on her doorstep for a quick session of bible bashing? Hear me crying, Lord, kum ba yah?'

'Okay, so what if I did? We evangelicals stick together, you know. She confided in me, so I was worried for her welfare. It was the least she deserved. Always prepared to stick her head above the parapet, that lady, and play up the importance of human dignity.'

'What d'you have in mind?'

'I mean her stall at the Christmas Bazaar, Inspector. Judith was the lynchpin of our annual fundraiser, selling Fair Trade coffee, handicrafts, and whatnot.'

Dárdai cocked a single bushy eyebrow, but did not deign to comment. 'So *you*, I take it, are the deceased's housekeeper?' He gave the girl a disparaging nod.

'Yessir,' she peeped, lips curled into a dutiful smile. 'I'm Melissa. Melissa Rawal.'

'So when did you arrive at your employer's house, Miss Rawal?'

'Eh . . . three pm as always, every Thursday, Saturday and Sunday.'

Dárdai's mouth twitched. 'Just a second. Are you *absolutely* sure?'

'Yes, I'm sure. Real sure. Three pm as always, every Thursday, Saturday . . .'

'And Sunday, or so you tell me, Miss Rawal. But isn't Sunday your day off?'

'No, sir.'

'And moving swiftly on, how is it that you were here for over four hours, but didn't notice that anything was amiss?'

'A Miss?'

'That anything was wrong,' clarified Dárdai petulantly.

'I have the keys, sir. I let myself in. Only went upstairs to clean the bathroom.'

'I see. Do you *always* have the keys, Miss Rawal? Every Thursday, Saturday . . .'

'And Sunday,' she interjected, evidently getting into her stride. 'I have them all the time. Just in case.'

'So, as far as you know, there've been no visitors to the house in the past twenty-four hours. Apart from yourself.'

'No,' avowed Rawal, shaking her head determinedly.

'I noticed a burglar alarm in the hall. Looked pretty new to me. How long had she had it?'

'Eh . . . about two weeks.'

'I see. When you showed yourself in, was it active or inactive?'

'I typed in the alarm code, innit?'

'You mean you disarmed the deceased's burglar alarm?'

'Yessir.'

'Look at me when I'm talking to you. That's better. So you assumed that she was out?'

'Out, sir? No, I thought she was having a kip. I didn't want to disturb her.'

'I see. Tell me, Miss Rawal: over the past fortnight, did

your employer often leave the alarm on downstairs even when she was in the house?'

'Eh . . . yes, I think so.'

'Even during the day?'

'Yes.'

From the far corner of the room, Dr. Popham swept the dust from his overalls in one grandiose gesture. 'Died early this morning. Anything between six am and seven am.'

'Substantial algor mortis?'

'Stone-cold. 27.6 degrees, to be precise.'

'Fine. Anything else?'

'Putrefaction negligible. Purplish discolouration of the skin, fully consistent with the onset of livor mortis. Extensive pooling of blood in lower portion of body, equally consistent with a faceup orientation.'

'You mean the body hasn't been moved?'

'Not recently. You'll observe, Dárdai, that the nightdress is speckled with blood, as is the dressing gown cord. I can't, as yet, find any signs of trauma in the neck region.'

'So *where* is all this blood from?' presented Dárdai. 'No obvious stab or bullet wounds?'

'None at all,' said Popham pontifically. 'Only this.' He held aloft a blister pack marked **COUMADIN®**. 'I found this in the bottom drawer of her bedside table.'

'Warfarin?'

'Bang on. You'll find that most anticoagulants can be fully reversed with vitamin K. To quote the Sanborn Clinical Drugs Dictionary, "vitamin K underlies the hepatic synthesis of several blood coagulation factors." Otherwise, for the rapid reversal of severe bleeding, fresh frozen plasma – that is to say the fluid portion of one unit of human blood that has been centrifuged, separated and frozen solid at minus eighteen degrees centigrade – can be administered to the patient.'

Dárdai doubled up. 'Cut the crap, Pop! If I needed to know *that*, I'd never have joined the Force.'

'What I'm intimating,' said the pathologist edgily, 'is that the means of rescue were ready and waiting. If only the deceased had phoned for an ambulance.'

'So why didn't she?' probed Dárdai. 'Was it suicide? Or was she held under duress?'

'Or merely the victim of an accidental overdose,' returned Popham. 'The deceased was elderly, of slim build and under five-foot-four, so at the lowest percentile of blood volume. Vulnerable to drug overdoses. If a surfeit of warfarin triggered a brain haemorrhage, she might've been dead within minutes of being symptomatic. So disorientated in the final stages of haemoptysis, she never made it to the phone.'

'Haemoptysis?'

'The coughing up of bright red, foamy blood from the respiratory tract. Common in the final throes of lung cancer and tuberculosis . . . and warfarin overdose.'

'Perhaps the brain haemorrhage blunted some of her pain.'

'Pure conjecture, Dárdai. First I'll need to cart her off to the labs: dazzle her with a burst or two of UV light.

Should've finished imaging hair and nail samples by midday tomorrow. You two are late, by the way.'

The forensic photographers looked suitably embarrassed as they removed their cumbersome Pentax K1000s from their PVC cases. Suffice to say, the room was now more crowded than at any point in its history.

Dárdai's stare carried annihilative force. 'How the fucking Jeeves are you two going to capture blood spatter patterns like that? Is that a lens or a cataract? Use some cleaning solvent! Hello, what have we here?'

Reflected in the dressing table mirror, beside an unopened box of throat lozenges, lay a buckram-bound book. With a crackle of spine stitching, Dárdai opened the volume at the flyleaf. For the first time since its appearance on an undergraduate reading list, he clasped a copy of Alexis de Tocqueville's *Democracy in America*. An English translation. The oblique alignment of its History Faculty Library stamp, last dated 17/3/10, hinted at a hurried issue desk withdrawal. A bookmark flitted out of the blackened inner pages. Had he stooped to retrieve it, he might have overlooked the three red asterisks in the verso margin.

Popham tried to expedite proceedings. 'What is it?'

'Page three hundred. She's highlighted a passage.'

The pathologist craned his neck for a better angle, coughed, and began to verbalise in the spiritless fashion that was his trademark: '"The world which is rising into existence is still half encumbered by the remains of the world which is waning into decay." Dramatic stuff, Dárdai.'

'And possibly significant, at least as a glimpse into the oppressed mindset that so often precedes suicide. Tenuous, I'll give you that, but we'd be foolish to discount the possibility. Don't suppose you buy it?'

Popham chuckled chestily. 'Short of reading the mind of the deceased, I'm in no position to offer a concrete answer. Hate speculation in all its . . .'

'But it's a *library* book,' broke in Travis. 'Lots of folks could have gotten it defaced! And even if Judith *did* make a few markings, you gotta try to enter her stream of consciousness. Like my tutor back at Yale, Judith had a mighty good brain on her, Inspector. Take it from me: mighty good. And quit with the belittling,' he snapped, as Dárdai puffed out his cheeks like a blowfish. 'By highlighting that passage, wasn't she doing the sensible thing and putting *Democracy in America* in the context of its time?'

'No man is an island, entire of itself,' recited Dárdai.

'You make it sound so trite,' rasped Travis, resenting the interruption. 'Remember, Inspector, that the Frenchman wrote at a crossroads in US history. Of high birth and a European, he believed he was taking the view of a dispassionate outsider. You gotta understand that when Tocqueville speaks of two worlds, he's talking about the impact of Jacksonian Democracy on the fabric of American life; the implosion of old-world aristocracy; the whys and wherefores of Manifest Destiny; the polarising potential of the slavery debate; the impending bloodbath of Civil War. Why presume suicide, Inspector? Besides, she would never take her own life. Way too devout for that.'

Dárdai's analytical mind processed the new information. Scowling fiercely, he opted for an untried tactic.

'The pathologist's résumé suggests no involvement on your part, Miss Rawal. Give us your statement and you're free to go. Oh, and one more thing,' he added ominously. 'Where can I locate her next of kin?'

The cleaner gazed at him with all the blankness of an Inuit pitilessly dumped in the souqs of Dar-es-Salaam. Still weakened by Saturday's *Quinta de la Rosa* tasting at Standlake's Wine Warehouse, Dárdai was at a loss to explain Rawal's behaviour. Speech seemed to issue from her larynx without involving the higher centres of her brain. Silence and sound: a golden ratio. Had she been seized by self-consciousness? That was certainly plausible. Or was her gormlessness a smoke-screen? If so, what was she hiding?

To his relief, something began to register in her weary terracotta orbs.

'She . . . she didn't speak to me about these things, but a friend once told me she had no close family. Just some cousins in France.' She pointed to the side-table beside the curtained window. 'Sent her that lava lamp last Christmas, innit?'

'I see,' returned Dárdai, biting his lip. 'And can you confirm what the deceased did for a living?'

'Taught at one of the colleges. Now which one wazzit?' The girl scratched her head cloddishly, eyes glued to the carpet, cudgelling her brains. As Dárdai turned to face her, he noticed – through several skeins of seal-brown hair – that a hearing aid was planted unobtrusively in her right ear. 'Oh yeah, I've remembered. It's Tresingham, sir. Defo Tresingham.'

PART THREE

CHAPTER NINE

'For good or ill, this was the domain of a man keen to prove that all tastes but his own were repellent.'

Beset by weakness, Zolotov clambered out of his kingsize leather bed. He'd been ripped from his slumber by the telltale signs of sinusitis: a searing pain between the eyes; thick, purulent nasal discharge; a dull headache that worsened on bending. Adamant that his ailment was of bacterial origin, he opened the chrome medicine cabinet in his glass-tiled bathroom. On the third shelf, behind the rechargeable rotary shaver, stood a plastic receptacle labelled *Родиола розовая*. With the aid of pincers, he broke the seal on his imported cache of Siberian Rhodiola. Bleary-eyed, bladder bursting, he gulped down a single capsule of the golden root extract.

His discomfort was compounded by a failure to locate his iTunes Account Information. He could have sworn he'd left the hard copy beside his keyboard, or slipped it beneath his coiled 3G earphones. Three filing cabinets and seven box-files later, he remained no closer to unearthing the elusive A4 sheet.

Dárdai's mid-morning telephone call came as a welcome diversion. Olsten had died within the stated range: at around 6.40 am according to Dr. Popham. She'd been formally identified with the help of a passport. Moleskin-bound, it gave the holder's surname as 'Olsten', her nationality as 'British', and her date of birth as '19.10.35'. A silver-mounted violin bow, marked with a single nick in the lower mortise, had been confined to a bedroom closet. A shameless fumble through the bathroom bin had yielded no fewer than seven yellow-stained incontinence pads. The Dame, Dárdai conjectured, had either surrendered all fear of losing face as she hastened her passage to heaven, or had died so unexpected a death that the idea of a posthumous house search hadn't even crossed her mind. Favouring the mental balm that came with a verdict of suicide, Dárdai clung obstinately to the first scenario.

Fixed to Olsten's fridge was a neatly written note:

> *'Hey Miss Olsten! Sorry I missed ya. Scrubbed bathroom, but ran outta time for kitchen floor. Hoovered lounge. Cleaned plates. Tried to feed Tuxedo his Vit E supps, but he didn't wanna know! See ya Thursday. Melissa XX'*

Olsten's burglar alarm had last been deactivated at 3.01pm. The date was logged as 11/04/10, elegantly corroborating Rawal's preliminary statement. Her fingerprints – deposited on the keypad via dermal secretions – had been rendered visible with the aid of a developer. The chemical reagent had revealed a second pair of fingerprints, shown to belong to the pensioner herself. If a third person had attempted to deactivate the alarm during a forced entry, it was safe to conclude that their hands were gloved.

The fire-resistant safe had seemed ill at ease with its milieu. It stood beside a three-kilowatt immersion heater at the back of an airing cupboard. Little attempt had been made to conceal its whereabouts from the opportunist thief, as if Olsten had reasoned thus: 'what use is there in a joist-bolted floor safe when a loose-fitting one is as hernia-inducing as it is impenetrable?' Ingress to the safe had proved troublesome, its elaborate boltwork precluding a machineless entry. Finding the LCD keypad positively unhelpful, Dárdai had been about to cut the Gordian knot by summoning a team of forensic engineers. Constable Ronald Gregson had diffidently put paid to *that* idea, suggesting that they focus on finding the manual override key. Fifty-five minutes later, and the ecstatic bobby was holding it aloft, until recently interspersed with potpourri. Humbled by his colleague's display of lateral thinking, Dárdai opened the safe, slid in a gloved hand, and extracted the following: a NatWest credit card, a birth certificate, and an assortment of jewellery.

Of moderate interest was a violet journal: the February issue of the *British Journal for the History of Philosophy*. Spanning pages 182 to 195 inclusive was an article entitled 'Visions of Utopia: Prince M. M. Shcherbatov and Inequality'. The Magyar was unsurprised to learn that Professor Dame Olsten was listed as its author, or that a succession of preprints – marked D, E and F in thick red ink – slid out of the glossy trimonthly. All standard practice. A line-by-line perusal revealed only slight differences between the versions: the removal of an intensifier; the addition of a footnote; some grammatical streamlining. The question he failed to ask was this: if drafts D, E and F were close at hand, what fate had befallen A, B and C?

All things considered, DCI Dárdai was satisfied that neither clergyman, nor cleaner, warranted further interrogation. Until the forensic position was established by Dr. Popham, watchful waiting would be the order of the day.

*

By the time Miss Mowbray, Zolotov's trusted housekeeper, had shown herself in at 10.55 am, he'd shaved, showered, annihilated three hemp bars, washed down a mug of Darjeeling Oolong, gargled with diluted TCP, hoovered his bed-sheets, dismembered the corrugated fibreboard cushioning his newly arrived VDU, locked the front door, and refitted the two lightweight roof panels stowed in his Porsche's front luggage compartment. On the unofficial orders of Dárdai, he was off to college. Olsten's college.

*

By quarter past eleven, Zolotov found himself opposite the Oxford University Museum of Natural History. Figueroa stood beside him in a two-piece suit. A notice outside Tresingham's gatehouse informed them that the College Library would be inaccessible until June. It gave the reason as 'unforeseen delays in restoration work'.

Zolotov nodded at a gangling student in the process of affixing his bike to a wall rack. 'That, by the way, is the unfortunately named Leonardo Clutterbuck,' he muttered, well within earshot of the student. 'Stays put during the Easter Vac, no? Off to Granada Studios next Tuesday to fly the Tresingham flag on University Challenge. Opted for the Yeltsin paper against the advice of his tutor, namely me, and duly paid the price. Only last week, the imbecile emailed me an essay on the 1993 Russian Constitutional Crisis, the point at which Yeltsin's confrontations with parliament reached their destructive climax. Commandeering tanks to shell the Russian White House, dear old Boris quite literally blasted his opponents out of parliament.'

'Should I find that remarkable?'

'It was a most cogent essay, Rena, as far as it went. Only Mr. Clutterbuck was under the impression that our chronic chuckler had punched holes in a rather different executive mansion. A Clinton-occupied Oval Office razed to the ground by Russian tanks? Paxman won't know whether to laugh or to cry.'

As it happened, neither did Figueroa.

The porter's lodge was fitted with a CCTV system, two omnidirectional microphones integrated into each camera. But the stacked pigeonholes fell outside their visual fields. Zolotov withdrew his Bod card and began to manipulate it in the manner of a practiced pen spinner. Friction and sweat had worn away the reader number which would otherwise have appeared beneath the barcode. Seeing no nearby porter, he repocketed it immediately.

'There's a curious anecdote about our locale which might, just *might*, amuse you.'

Despite an inquiring turn of the head, Figueroa continued to drift distractedly along the paved walkway. Fringed with bluebells and purple azaleas, it culminated in a vast quadrangle subdivided into grass segments. She could only marvel at how the sunken lawn accentuated the soaring vertices of nearby buildings.

'On its construction in 1867,' began the Russian, fastening the top button of his speckless black shirt, 'Tresingham was thoroughly despised by the University, most of all by nearby Lindmouth from which it had purchased land. A secret society was founded in protest of the college's pioneering reliance on Gothic Revival, no? To enter, legend has it, one had to forcibly remove a brick and present it to the society's elders. Ordinary membership required the removal of a red brick, higher-level membership a somewhat rarer white brick, chairmanship a blue brick. The hope was that Tresingham would be wiped off the face of this earth. A touch optimistic, think you not?'

'Very funny,' groaned Figueroa, rolling her dark eyes in incredulity. 'But I suspect you're pulling my leg.'

Ambivalent on how best to respond, Zolotov sharpened

his gaze on a gargoyle projecting from the chapel's sandstone gutter. Rainwater gurgled through its grotesquely carved throat. A howl of anathema in an unknown tongue? A warning to those of malign intent? The bane of an ancient evil? When his answer came, it did so as a flavourless avowal. 'In this case, Rena, not at all.'

The calm was punctured by a sombre whirr: Bach's Passacaglia and Fugue in C Minor. Figueroa found the organ pleasantly beguiling. Having auditioned for several music conservatoires back in Buenos Aires, she was familiar with the Baroque repertoire. How she yearned to pass beneath the chapel's archway, settle down in a transept pew, and devour the virtuosic variations beyond the eight-bar ground bass. But persuading Zolotov to delay his inquiry would be a lost cause. The Russian, she'd come to learn, had scant interest in all things ecclesiastical. Musings on the subject of church spires would, with astounding regularity, elicit a verbatim regurgitation of Virgil: 'If I cannot bend Heaven, I shall move Hell'. And it didn't end there. Only last week, her supervisor had been far from jocular when displeasuring her with: 'God demands spiritual fruit, not religious nuts'. When asked for his views on Eastern Orthodoxy, he'd replied in three words, two of which had been 'Eastern Orthodoxy!' Piety was strictly out, as were passacaglias. She'd do well to shelve her earlier plans.

'If my memory serves me correctly,' said Zolotov, ambling past the frescoed entrance to the College Library, 'the Master's lodgings should be here. Ni'aha!'

They stopped by a heavy door. Engraved in its brass

plaque, vastly emboldened, were the words: 'PROFESSOR R. GERSHMAN, MASTER'. What might have been uncluttered floorspace had been carelessly overlaid with a dust sheet. Restoration work, no doubt. Having swallowed his mango jelly bean in exasperation, Zolotov adjusted his silk tie. He knocked twice, sharply.

A muffled 'Come' meandered its way through a pulsating klezmer dance. Trill upon trill of warbling clarinet solo, all locked in a melodic mode of supplication. Cimbalom and woodblock first anticipated, then trailed, the duple oom-pah beat, at which point the accordion, till now dissonant, prompted a harmonic resolution. 'A discharge of surplus neural tension', as Zolotov's first research supervisor might have put it.

Gershman was resplendent in suede shoes and a polo-necked sweater. Thrown over was a crisp orange blazer: plain brass buttons, no crests. His hair was as black as his eyebrows, barring some sprinklings of white at the tips of his sideburns. The weedy frame was matched by a wizened complexion. It bore an uncanny resemblance to the skin of a Habanero chilli: sundried, then pickled in vinegar and brine.

His room was a tableau of Victorian sophistication. Green lace antimacassars covered every chairback. The striped walls were bestudded with paintings and prints. Zolotov recognised a reproduction of the oil-on-canvas original he'd seen at Tate Britain only a month ago: Turner's *Peace - Burial at Sea*. The arched windows were rimmed by pleated taffeta curtains, gold tassels lending them an air of fussy distinction. A globular blue lamp stood on a rosewood desk; the type used for light therapy. It was flanked by two millefiori paperweights, eyelike and multicoloured. For good or ill, this was the domain of a man keen to prove that all tastes but his own were repellent.

The adjoining room told a very different story. It was utilitarian rather than elegant, comprising a sink, mirror, single bed and futon to boot. From the apparent absence of a specialised music system, Zolotov deduced that Gershman had been listening to Der Heyser Bulgar via his laptop.

Figueroa shut the door, a little too forcefully. The Master's wily brown eyes slewed from one unfamiliar face to the other. With an urgency suggestive of guilt or abashment, he shut the lid of his laptop and placed it roughly in the desk drawer. Then he waited.

'No handshake, huh?' Figueroa's boldness bordered on insolence.

'Might get one when you've told me who you are,' returned the Master coarsely.

Zolotov thought it wise to intercede on her behalf. 'I work for DCI Dárdai, Thames Valley Police. The name's Zolotov, and this is Dr. Figueroa. You may wish to remain seated, Professor, for we come as the bringers of sad news.'

'Oh really?' said Gershman sourly, revealing two crooked rows of tobacco-stained teeth. 'What could *possibly* be worse than all this repair work. Damn irksome!'

'Quite a lot, actually. A don of yours, Dame Olsten, was found dead in bed on Sunday evening.'

Gershman's spirit seemed shaken – for a full three seconds. 'How do you know all this?' he lisped, his speech defect rendering every 's' a 'th'.

'Never mind that,' intoned Zolotov, his voice menacingly soft. 'A stalwart Tresophyte is dead. Suicide? Accidental overdose? We endeavour to find out. Cooperate with us, Gershman, and the police will drift between your Common Rooms like the feathery pappi of a pollinating *Cirsium arvense.* Prevaricate, and you risk . . .'

'You're threatening me?'

'You *could* say that.'

'I see,' replied the other leadenly, pouring what looked like cranberry juice into a glass. 'As I have nothing to hide, you might as well sit down. Wouldn't want you to think me inhospitable.'

Figueroa promptly sank her frame into a balloon back chair. Zolotov chose to stand, gemstone glistening.

'Olsten was top-drawer in her professional capacity, no?'

The Master smiled, a little too deliberately. 'The doyenne of our SCR, you understand. She filled many a room with her presence. Always well groomed. Still as stiff as a ramrod.'

Zolotov thought the imagery a little gauche, but opted to keep his own counsel.

'A formidable woman,' continued Gershman. 'Rarely one to lavish praise on anybody. Whenever she *did*, we thought it a red-letter day.' He paused to appraise the impact of his words. Sensing none, he proceeded in a level baritone. 'I speak as a former student of hers – studied PPE here in the seventies. To say she was loquacious would be something of an understatement. She was – how shall I put this politely? – rather too inebriated with the exuberance of her own verbosity, if you get my drift.'

'Naturally,' chuckled Zolotov, resettling his glasses on his aquiline nose. 'Who on *earth* do you take me for?' He sounded more amused than affronted.

'Judith, as I was about to point out, adored Formal Hall. It was here, at Tresingham High Table, that I believe I last saw her. Yes, that's it – her good friend Dr. Rae was among the attendees. Dinner last Tuesday.' Gershman lowered his voice. 'She's the economist with the chronic halitosis; frightfully bad breath in simple English. Poor woman – if only she knew.'

'Rae?' verified Zolotov, opening his PDA and inputting the name with a stylus. His command of palmtop shorthand remained a work in progress.

'Correct. Not that I've ever been one for schmaltz, you understand.'

Zolotov's face barely flickered. 'You refer to maudlin sentimentality?'

'Plainly.' The Master withdrew an angular pair of reading glasses from his cigar-shaped case. 'Come to think of it, nor was Dame Olsten. A Professor Emeritus in Enlightenment Ontology. Emeritus, but by no means close to surrendering all the duties implied in her former title. Whether Judith was ever chagrined at not holding a chair endowed by a benefaction, I really couldn't say. Still, she held a personal professorship from 1981 to 2005, a tenured position with all the job security and intellectual autonomy that one entails.' He sighed. 'Senior professors so often find themselves on the margins of productivity, proving quite unworthy of the confidence placed in them by their employers. Judith, mind you, never outgrew her usefulness. Seems like only yesterday she co-edited *The Identity of Indiscernibles: A Symposium.* That followed *Leibniz and Salva Veritate: Truth-value Revisited.* Of late, she'd been dabbling with . . .'

'Shcherbatov?' Zolotov suggested gently.

Gershman nodded, his 'yes' almost inaudible. 'Olsten still gave occasional master-classes. Not a mainstay in Oxford jargon, I hasten to add.'

'I know,' said the Russian testily. 'Been an Oxonian for a quarter of a century.'

'Forgive me,' back-pedalled the Master. 'Which college?'

'I'm ubiquitous, though I regard Clapperton as my anchor. You were saying.'

'Indeed I was. Some weeks back, Judith approached me about an anonymous letter. The poison pen variety. Said she'd found it in her pigeonhole one afternoon after orchestra practice. Asked me to keep the matter confidential.'

'And why do you think she did *that*, Professor?'

'Isn't it obvious?' bristled Gershman. 'The Dame wanted to avoid a scandal, personal and collegiate. Nothing to be gained from telling colleagues, particularly when razor blades were involved. Stainless steel disposables. Four of them. Judging by the absence of hair, I conclude that they were almost certainly unused.'

Zolotov gulped down a gasp. 'Razor blades, you say? Not quite the frolics of a female student. Or perhaps that's all part of the bluff, no?'

'Frolics, you say? Nothing more sinister?'

'Very much doubt it. But I should like to see the note.'

Aware that he was outnumbered two to one, Gershman hesitated before replying. 'And what do you plan on doing with it, eh?'

'Good question,' deadpanned Zolotov. A gleam of mischief quickened in his eyes. 'Short of reading it, I suppose I could always entrust it to the Nippon Origami Museum in that inimitable City of Kaga. Then again, if the mood so takes me, I could subject it to paper chromatography in the hope of unveiling the hidden colours in maple leaves. Better still, I could . . .'

'In *that* case,' interjected the Master, 'I'll go and retrieve it from the porter's safe.'

Yet Gershman still had misgivings about his visitors, for rather than leaving them in the outmoded comfort of his office, he eyed them askance, rose to his feet, manufactured some excuse about college security, and ushered them back into the oak-panelled corridor. He took tangible delight in double-locking his door, before setting off for the porter's lodge without another word.

They sat at extreme ends of a paint-flecked wooden bench. The Russian studied the floor, cleft chin sagging against his chest. Figueroa held her head high, arms folded, rapt in tacit conjecture.

'A sensitive theme,' began Zolotov, chewing the cud of psychoanalysis, 'but how does one begin to enter the mind of a self-killer?'

Figueroa rolled her head airily, russet fringe dappling silky brow. 'A sense of nihility; of living in a void. The feeling that nothing or nobody, however well-meaning, can halt the cycle of self-denigration and despair. Why? Because their lives are devoid of a key ingredient.'

'And what would *that* be?'

'Friendship, Konstantin. The sum total of amity, constancy and core human decency. Affection that extends beyond a desire for copulation.'

'Which makes me wonder . . .'

'Which makes *me* wonder,' lanced through Figueroa, 'what desperate soul attends a college dinner just days before killing themselves?'

'Peculiar, think you not?'

'Very. Dárdai never mentioned a suicide note?'

'None was found.'

'Hardly surprising, I suppose. Olsten was an elderly spinster with no family in England. Dárdai said so. To whom would she leave a note?'

Zolotov levered himself up from the bench. 'My point entirely, Rena. Gershman implied she was the intrepid type, no?'

'Too intrepid and self-assured to succumb to suicidal thoughts, you mean?'

'Perhaps. Ni'aha! *S Rozhdestvóm!*'

Zolotov had spotted Gershman emerging from a side door. His brisk, regular gait suggested that he was well apprised of the value of time. One hand clasped a creased envelope; the other was planted in a deep trouser pocket. His manner conveyed an inner composure, certain that what he now held would hasten the end of this unwelcome exchange. He motioned them back into his office with a roll of the head.

'For remote viewing only,' he declared, holding the envelope as if it were a sizzling firecracker. Peering over Gershman's shoulder, Figueroa surveyed it with solicitous eyes. By the absence of a stamp, address or postmark, she concluded that the envelope had been delivered by hand. But by whom? By someone who remained at large – that much was clear. By someone who might, even now, be tracking their every move. Despite the protection afforded by Gershman's office walls, she felt a sickening lurch in the pits of her stomach.

While dog-eared, the note itself was tastefully penned in dark blue ink.

We know you, Dame Olsten. You don't know US, but WE know YOU! We know what you did and chose NOT to do.

Watch your step, Dame Olsten! Your days are numbered.

NO MORE SAFE HAVENS ...

'Quite unnerving, huh?' remarked Figueroa. 'Must have come as a real shock to her.'

'Certainly, but is this everything?' probed Zolotov. 'Any envelopes through her letterbox? Any anonymous telephone calls?'

'Not that she was prepared to share with me,' lisped Gershman, pushing his reading glasses to the top of his forehead. 'Then again, Judith wasn't quite as perturbed by the whole affair as one might expect.'

'How very odd. Any idea what might have warranted this?'

'None whatsoever. When I asked her about it, Judith said she didn't know. She admitted, to her credit, that certain students had every reason to find her a touch overbearing, but struggled to identify anyone who might wish her dead.' He squeezed his Adam's apple. 'Isn't it odd how someone in the third millennium should resort to the antiquated method of handwriting? Typing the note on, say, a library computer would have been far less incriminating.'

'*Less* incriminating, you say? We'll come to that later. First thing you ought to know is that this isn't handwriting as such.'

'What the devil do you mean?'

'The script, you'll observe, is unnatural in its regularity. Unless I'm very much mistaken, it mimics the Lucida typeface in Microsoft Word. A distinctive series of garland strokes, more Calligraphy than Blackletter. Notice the slight projections that complete each upstroke? These serifs are particularly visible in the upper-case 'T' and 'H', think you not?'

Gershman nodded slowly. 'The writing implement appears to have pierced the page on . . . let's see now . . . *five* occasions. Please explain.'

'Written in a torrent of fury,' offered Figueroa, her sense of danger spiralling. 'A forward slant suggestive of high emotional expressiveness. A monstrous libido!'

'Perhaps,' uttered Zolotov, cringing slightly. 'Or the result of transferring our typeface from an overlaid piece of tracing paper. Our writer has attempted to follow the contours of "Dame", but has done so very inexactly.'

'Quite,' concurred Gershman. 'One wonders why they didn't just type the note.'

'Because doing so would have been far more incriminating.'

'Please explain.'

'Gladly. As any apprentice steganographer will tell you, high-end laser printers leave artefacts on the printed page: fine, almost invisible, yellow dots. These tiny dots contain encoded printer serial numbers, time stamps, and so on. By shrewd deduction, investigators can narrow their ring of suspects. They can even trap their man.'

Figueroa clapped her hands. 'Or woman!'

'Just a figure of speech, Doctor. And I'm sure you'll agree that women are equally, if not more, capable of such diablerie.' He refocused his attention on the Master. 'Isn't it odd how little substance weaves its way onto that page?

It's swarming with ambiguities and implicit threats, but discloses very little. Nothing about paying money with menaces. No "we know where you live, Dame Olsten", though a literal construal of "no more safe havens" may amount to the same thing. All in all, an intriguing choice of language.'

'What did you have in mind?'

'For instance,' drawled Zolotov, as if endowed with all the time in the world, 'are we from the word "more" in "no more safe havens" to infer some shared history between Olsten and our writer? Or is that all part of the game?'

Gershman's eyes narrowed. 'You speak of the writer in the singular. How, then, do you account for the "we"?'

'Classic device used by blackmailers, my friend. A cunning ploy to appear more threatening, whilst simultaneously throwing the spotlight on group motives should an inquiry be launched. Enough to lead a trainee criminologist up the gum tree.'

'More twaddle!' cried Gershman. 'How can you possibly be so certain? Bring me a professional graphologist! A specialist in handwriting analysis!'

Zolotov blinked twice. 'Graphologist? Whatever happened to modern-day forensics? Please understand that subjecting a computer trace to graphological analysis is about as helpful as fishing for gristle in an all-soya-meat ragoût. If you want specific findings, focus your search on fingerprints.'

'And what if they wore gloves?' The lines deepened on Gershman's prominent forehead.

'Then we explore other routes: incriminating trace fibres, grease stains, smatterings of salivary DNA on the envelope's flap. Anastasiya, my ex-wife, knows a thing or two about that. Now a consultant haematologist at Chelsea and Westminster Hospital, or so she tells me.' His eyes moved uneasily towards the futon in the adjoining room. 'I, meanwhile, never truly embraced science at the molecular level. Not quite. Anything else, Professor?'

'I was about to ask you the same question.'

'Patience, my friend! Patience. Oh, and about that lamp on your desk. What is its purpose, precisely?'

Gershman dabbed at his nose with a handkerchief. 'Research indicates that a very specific wavelength of blue light may assist in combating afternoon sluggishness by suppressing melatonin production in the brain. This year my SAD appears to have spilt over into the spring, what with the weather being so foul.'

'Schizoaffective disorder?' discharged Zolotov, now thoroughly enjoying himself.

Gershman shook his head irritably.

'Separation anxiety disorder?' volunteered Figueroa, riding the wave of sarcasm.

'Seasonal affective disorder, actually. Most people infer my meaning from the meteorological context. Polar angles aside, there are a thousand reasons why my wife and I prefer to spend our winters on sub-equatorial beaches, and *not* in the saddles of Lapland mares.' He transfixed them with a steely stare. 'We all have our foibles; our imperfections. This just so happens to be mine.'

'How refreshing to hear you say so!' gushed Zolotov. 'I've always maintained that if humans had no foibles, they wouldn't derive so much pleasure from seeing them exhibited in others, no?'

Gershman couldn't bring himself to say 'speak for yourself', but an overt scowl made for a worthy substitute.

'Blue light?' resumed Zolotov with interest. 'I could have *sworn* it was more cyan than blue.'

The Master gave him a lopsided smirk. 'The reason for that illusion is no great mystery. Have you considered parting company with those?'

If an unbroken line could have been traced from Gershman's forefinger, it would have collided with the rubberised nosebridge of Zolotov's spectacles.

'These?' spluttered the Russian, irises aflame in umbrage. 'There's as much chance of me disowning *these* as of me hiring a Mir submersible to recover the Potemkin!'

Gershman frowned indulgently. 'Yes, yes, but wasn't it blown to smithereens by the interventionists in Sevastopol? To prevent it from falling into Bolshevik hands?'

'Naturally – Krupp armour, conning tower and all.' With the PDA stylus, Zolotov tapped his nosebridge in time with the metrical stress of his words. 'My point entirely, Professor Gershman.'

And barely eight miles away, in Culham Science

Centre's F5 building, under the probing gaze of a morgue attendant, Dr. Popham spotted a signature bulge in his cadaver's chest. The four-centimetre elevation could mean only one thing: Dame Olsten had been fitted with an artificial pacemaker.

CHAPTER TEN

'"There exists a fine line between knowing the ropes and finding yourself on the end of one, no?"'

By quarter to three, Zolotov was back in Flat 17B. Moments earlier, he'd deposited Figueroa outside Clapperton's main gates – her rent-free lodgings – before driving home to Summertown. On entering the hall, his nasal hairs were awakened by a heady scent: Miss Mowbray's Lancashire hotpot. It might have been headier still had his sinusitis been less ingrained.

A Sony Ericsson was bleeping. *His.* Not a call as such, but a text from Dárdai:

HOW WAS MASTER? TRESINGHAM? NEED INFO ASAP. BIG BACKLOG OVER HERE. DUE IN COURT 4 TIMES NEXT WEEK, SO LOADS OF EVIDENCE TO BRUSH UP ON. SUPT CLEAVER IS GETTING RATTY AND I MUST ADMIT, SO AM I. YOU WERE A LOT MORE CUT AND THRUST AT UNI WHEN DEADLINES WERE DEADLINES. WHAT'S CHANGED? OKAY, SILLY QUESTION. BUT NO DAWDLING, OKAY!

Having decanted all surface grease, Zolotov spooned out a generous helping of Miss Mowbray's *chef d'œuvre* – no point in contacting Dárdai until he'd had time to order his thoughts. He carried his plate into the lounge, turned on the Sony BRAVIA, and selected Bloomberg Europe. He was aggrieved to learn that each of his 5000 shares in Albika plc had plummeted from 345 to 313 pence in under a fortnight. How far, he wondered, had the proposed outsourcing of operations architecture to agencies in Bangkok flattened investor confidence? Had shareholders panicked in response to alleged malpractice investigations into power utility markets? Halfway through muttering that old adage – 'you cannot catch a falling knife' – the suit-clad Russian succumbed to the forces of fatigue.

He awoke refreshed and in better spirits – a sea change comparable to that undergone by a Koryak shaman after quaffing a liquid quart of some rare hallucinogenic fungus. Rolling back his sleeve, he stared at the oddball watch financed by his REES colleagues. Its numberless, handless face served as the gridiron for a tiny ball bearing; one that rolled around at the slightest provocation. He held it as he would a compass: perfectly still, parallel to the plane of the floor. Gradually, guardedly, a magnet dragged the silver orb into position. 19:10, he estimated. With only one ball to denote hours as well as minutes, some degree of approximation was inevitable.

Slipping on his orange moccasins, Zolotov ambled over to his computer desk. He jiggled the mouse. The Google homepage appeared in place of his Animated

Russian Proverbs screensaver. He hesitated, then typed 'facebook.com' into the blank search box. Before long, its familiar sign-up page materialised, prompting him to input his email address and password. He entered 'kzolotov@clapperton.ox.ac.uk' into the first box, 'scriabin1872' into the one below.

After much deliberation, Zolotov had joined the Facebook community in Michaelmas, 2009. Figueroa had appealed to his curiosity by highlighting the boons of the pitiless News Feed.

'Glorified snooping,' she'd called it. 'You can keep tabs on anyone, anytime, anywhere, and no-one will know you're doing it! And guess what? There's even a Russian version!'

Zolotov had capitulated, ostensibly to convey a sense of receptivity to all things modern, truly to be left in peace. A part of him, however small, detested the idea of younger colleagues being better connected than their seniors. But within days of joining, he was floundering in a barrel of kitsch features and inane third-party applications. 'What kind of hobo are you?' and 'How ghetto are you?' – to name but a few – lay comfortably beyond the pale of Zolotovian participation.

As of today, his own notifications box was empty: no new messages, no event invitations, no friend requests, no pokes. Unoffended, he typed 'Delia Holdenby' into a search box to the left of the main interface. It yielded three results: a Delia Y. Holdenby on the JPMorgan Chase network, a Mira Holdenby from Calgary, and his deceased subject, Delia

J. Holdenby, South East England. Success. He clicked tentatively on the last name and waited.

Right where a blue-grey silhouette appeared on his own profile, Delia had uploaded a photo. Judging by the thickness of her blonde curls, the healthy glow in her cheeks, the headshot had been taken well before the start of chemotherapy. Her smile illuminated every angular feature; a smile so undeserving of the card that fate had dealt her. As far as Zolotov could glean, no privacy settings had been applied to her profile. Groups, Gifts and the Wall were all accessible – for now at least. There was a deluge of messages from work colleagues, most of them female. Dabbing deftly at his scroll wheel, he browsed through all the mawkish stock references to 'shared staffroom gossip', 'devotion as an English teacher', 'selflessness'. The eighth message ended with a banal: 'whenever you entered a room, you filled it with your warmth'. Now where had he heard *that* before? No – his mistake. Julie Summers had written 'warmth'. Gershman had recounted Olsten's 'presence'. A world of difference.

Unaware of Delia's passing, a chum had subjected her to the Tease option on Hug Me. Either that, or Tim O'Gorman had a warped sense of humour. The second hypothesis would prove the more accurate, however, with O'Gorman proceeding to write: 'I *told* you the FTSE 100 would shimmy over the 5630 mark by the end of the month! Another misjudged bet!! ☺ !! Whichever side of life you're on, Delia, I'll be waiting for that Yorkie bar with bated breath, lol!'

Scrolling further down her Wall, he came across several tributes dated the 7th of April, 2010. The fifth one down kindled his interest:

Dear Mrs. Holdenby,

So very saddened to hear of your passing – the end came far too soon. When I visited you after the clinical trial, the gravity of your illness was plain to see; as was the strength of your Faith. You were ever-present at our Sunday services. You sat alone in the front pew, a model of piety. You found time for us; we found time for you. Health permitting, you would have continued to support us as your heart and mind dictated. May the rod and staff of the Lord buttress your loved ones in this trying time, and guide your immortal soul to the Kingdom of Heaven. May you rest in peace.

Reverend Travis Schiller

But as the seconds ticked by, the more uneasy Zolotov became. It wasn't Travis' remorseless religiosity that discomfited him – there, at least, the Texan was being true to type. Nor was it his possible insincerity: hollow words were in attendance at the most poignant funeral oration, in the warmest epitaph, in the most magnanimous condolence letter.

The Facebook shrine was a newcomer to the world of online ethics. Recent months had seen a surge of virtual memorials – portals into lives previously shuttered. To many, the e-shrine was a public book of condolence; a bastion of connectivity with the deceased; a bond between fellow mourners. Zolotov entertained a different view.

Here was a newfangled gizmo that jeopardised the vintage union between grief and gravestone; a dynamo behind the puerile shift from private homage to open adulation. It transformed the inquisitive surfer into an imposter, a busybody, a prier. His overwhelming impression was that it should remain the property of Delia's family. *Tochka.*

Pulse fluttering, Zolotov rose ponderously from the swivel chair. Blood rushed towards his numbed extremities. He lifted his suit jacket by its silk scruff and carried it through into the kitchen. A ring of recessed spotlights accentuated the striking lustre. Surface clutter was consigned to an island console, two sinks welded into its polished granite countertop.

While blessed with the dubious gift of reheatability, Miss Mowbray's hotpot had somehow lost its appeal. Zolotov fancied something lighter, cooler, blander. Opening the console doors, he withdrew a wooden chopping board and a tourne knife. Yes, the latter was rather blunter than he might have liked, but it would have to do. Sidling over to his fridge, he extracted a green-rinded cylindrical fruit which had cemented pride of place in the vegetable drawer: a cucumber. A burst of ingenuity had seen him salvage the top of a spray cream bottle. Its *raison d'être*? An improvised sheath to preserve the integrity of his exposed cucumber end.

'Life must be pretty idyllic if your happiness hangs on the freshness of a cucumber,' Figueroa had mocked, peering at this disturbingly prophylactic arrangement. 'Can it be true?'

'Now *that*, Rena, is nothing more than boilerplate!' he'd rejoined acerbically. 'Has it never occurred to you that my ritualistic immersion in a sea of minutiae might constitute a goal in itself? A quest for distraction not unlike that which prompts the purchase of an executive car valeting kit . . . or a box of medicated toothpicks.'

With that, he'd left in a blur of grey, white and green, humming the climactic bars of Danse Macabre for no conceivable reason. Figueroa had very wisely declined to comment.

Half a cucumber and eight rice crackers later, Zolotov re-entered the lounge. Driftless thoughts whirled through his mind. Passing the feature fire, he disengaged his Sony Ericsson from a DC connector and began to mount the staircase to his roof terrace. He tried, and ultimately failed, to ignore the bluster of voices issuing so inconsiderately from the bowels of Flat 17A. A familial squabble in full throttle, no doubt.

Sheets of chrome-edged glass bounded the wooden deck. Pure minimalism. Zolotov gazed at the darkening skyline, soon to be recast in a sublime, bluish glow. Globular clouds were amassing in rolls and clumps – an inverted sea of mackerel scales. Whorls of smoke belched from a nearby barbecue, thoroughly fused with the aroma of mown grass. The union might have been invigorating had his sense of smell been its usual acute self.

He dialled a number he knew by rote.

'Yep?' answered Dárdai on the third ring.

'Ni'aha!'

'And about time too,' snorted the DCI. 'Still at that seventies shithole they call HQ, I'm afraid.'

'Working the lobster shift?'

'But of course. Just heard back from the lab. Olsten's been screened for external abnormalities: hair samples, paint chips, textile fibres, fingernails, fingerprints. The upshot? No suspicious marks or secretions whatsoever.'

'*Should* there have been?'

'Put it this way, Zolotov. If our pastor – or indeed our cleaner – took the liberty of interfering with the Dame, you'd expect the incriminating evidence to speak for itself. So far it appears to be suffering from laryngitis.'

'Frightfully droll, Chief Inspector.'

'True to form. And there's progress on the toxicology front.'

'Warfarin in her bloodstream?'

'Yep. We await the clinching data, but appear to be dealing with a higher-than-medically-prescribed concentration. Odd in light of what her chemist said.'

'Go on,' drawled Zolotov, his curiosity whetted.

'The chemist confirmed that Olsten had been taking her new dose for exactly five days. Two tablets – the blue variety – were to be taken each evening. Now listen to this,' he added feverishly. 'The blister pack by her bedside was only a quarter empty. Ten tablets, and no more, had been taken.'

Hearing the word 'ten', Zolotov almost dropped his phone. 'Incredible!'

'Not necessarily. Popham reckons that Olsten fell behind

with her doses and took, say, eight in one go. Twenty-four mg, in other words.'

'Can't imagine eight killing her that fast. The body metabolises warfarin more slowly than most therapeutic drugs – one of the few things I gleaned from my eight months at the Leningrad Medical Institute, no?'

'That's what I thought until Popham brought my attention to the many drug-drug interactions involving warfarin; medications that enhance the action of the anticoagulant to life-threatening proportions. Aspirin, ibuprofen and the antiulcer drug cimetidine all stuck in my mind. Supplements are equally culpable. Pop tells me – and I'm looking down at my notes here – that chemists from the University of Wisconsin have found root ginseng and ginkgo biloba to markedly increase blood pressure. This may exacerbate internal bleeding, not least in patients on anti-clotting medications. Popham suspects that Olsten was taking supplements against the advice of her GP. Now dig this!'

'Dig what?'

'Just an expression, Zolotov. Dig the fact that following a heart attack in the summer of 1997, Olsten was fitted with an artificial pacemaker in Paris. Her post-mortem has confirmed the presence of such a device. Her GP filled me in on the history.'

'And so even a moderate warfarin overdose knocked her for six, so to speak?'

'Exactly.'

Zolotov filled his lungs with cool, humid air. 'But you'll agree, Dárdai, that there exists a fine line between *knowing* the ropes and finding yourself on the end of one, no?'

'Christ! More cerebral confetti!'

'Call it what you will. And about Delia Holdenby . . .'

'Cut-and-dried,' rumbled the Magyar. 'The Holdenby case is closed.'

'But am I correct in presuming that Delia's body was only given a 'view and grant'? A plain external examination?'

'You are.'

'Because the examiner decided that the cause and manner of her death was manifest? That an internal post-mortem would be superfluous?'

'But of course,' returned Dárdai, his voice barbed. 'Adequately supported by her medical records and the unique circumstances of her death.'

'Then dare I suggest that you cover all bases by ordering a *full* forensic post-mortem.'

'Go for the jugular, you mean?'

'Precisely.'

Dárdai downed his mug of instant coffee. 'Bloody well hope you're right, Zolotov. Unlike the Department of Education, Superintendent Cleaver cannot afford the luxury of euphemisms like "deferred success" and "critical performance re-levelling". Won't give a tsetse fly's fart about me once I'm off the case.'

'My point entirely,' chuckled Zolotov. 'And remember that all truth passes through three stages. First, it is ridiculed. Second, it is violently opposed. Third, it is accepted as self-evident. You're a solid 2.5, no?'

'Right now, I'm closer to a 1.5. Now where were we? Ah yes. Been in touch with the Holdenby family solicitor. Bent as a Kirby grip hairpin, but he seemed to know his stuff. Emerges Delia didn't have a life insurance policy in any way, shape or form. So much for your suggestion of foul play in the family.'

'Now you're putting words in my mouth, Dárdai. The whole rationale behind ordering a post-mortem is to ascertain precisely what went into Delia's veins at the Churchill. Was it the virus, and *only* the virus?'

'I expect we'll know soon enough. All in ample time for her funeral on Thursday morning.'

'And the officiating rector?'

'A certain Reverend Travis. And they're not in the habit of calling themselves rectors, Zolotov.'

'My apologies. Small world, think you not?'

'Got there before I did. The aforementioned Texan tells me he knew Delia reasonably well. Described her as a regular churchgoer; the sort who shows up at just about every function known to man: cream teas; fundraisers; Bach Vespers; induction services for new Reverends. Gave me some spiel about liturgical colours, namely on how Lutherans never change their stole colour from its appointed season.'

'Even for weddings and funerals?'

'Especially for weddings and funerals. Something to do with remembering that our joys and sorrows fall within all phases of life, apparently.'

'Interesting. Is Holdenby equally devout?'

'A militant atheist – the assessment of our favourite bible basher.'

'I see. Incidentally, has anyone at Thames Valley bothered to confirm Travis' movements on the morning Olsten died?'

Dárdai paused. 'Not as yet. But DS Jameson did speak to a Mr. McGillycuddy at New Inn Yard, the headquarters of 001 Taxis. Transpires he collected Reverend Travis from St Columba's United Reformed Church, and deposited him at . . .'

'No. 36 Cardigan Street,' pre-empted Zolotov. 'Did the driver have anything rip-roaring to report?'

Dárdai considered the question. 'Mr. McGillycuddy was surprisingly on the ball, Zolotov. By some freakish coincidence, it was he who answered Olsten's call at eleven-ten on Saturday evening. Picked her up from a semi-detached Abingdon residence and drove her the seven or so miles to Jericho. The bottom line is that when she entered No. 36, Olsten seemed hale and hearty. That was eleven-fifty.'

'Driving . . . driving . . . that reminds me. I'm due to pay a certain lady a visit.'

'Oh really,' said Dárdai with pointed interest. 'Who's the lucky lass?'

'Dr. Philomena Rae. Tresingham College.'

'Wait till it's dark, Zolotov. More . . . eh . . . romantic.'

A sharp switch from handset to loudspeaker. Then a static hiss.

'Nothing like that!' chortled Zolotov. 'From the way her college Master described her, namely her oral hygiene, I think I should be eternally grateful that my sinus infection has blunted my sense of smell.'

CHAPTER ELEVEN

'The smugness in her voice unsettled him: she knew too much.'

Zolotov opened his eyes to another pewter-toned morning. He was pleased to learn that the letterbox, so frequently barren, now harboured a gift-wrapped bottle of *Piper-Heidsieck Brut Vintage 1998*. Loosely adhered was an unsigned note, almost contrived in its coyness:

> *'Many thanks from us all. Further to last term's helpful feedback, we particularly value your advice on which lectures were missable and which were not. Enjoy! XXX'*

The script was understated and slightly aslant. He traced its origin to Fionnoula MacKenna, the flirtatious Dubliner who only last term had chalked up a nauseating fifty thousand words spanning eight essays. Worse still, she'd insisted on handwriting each of her opuses 'because that's how the examiners will see my final script, okay'. There'd been two blokes and Miss MacKenna in the Cold War tutorial group, so it followed naturally that *she*, and not the others, had taken pains to underline her indebtedness.

While the three 'kisses' were provocative to the point of indecency, it was her gesture that counted. Zolotov resolved to email his thanks.

After yet another vain rummage for his iTunes Account Information, he left for Summertown Group Practice, 160 Banbury Road. The young Jamaican receptionist directed him to an affable, if faintly effeminate, locum. Without further ado, the GP prescribed a course of amoxicillin and ample rest. The sinus complaint, he assured Zolotov, was unlikely to be chronic. In under a week, he could expect to grind the grist of life once more.

Unbeknown to the locum, Zolotov took each injunction with a degree of caution. Antibiotics were soporific, repose impractical. He would regard amoxicillin as no more than a fallback should his herbal arsenal fail him. Right now, he needed his faculties sharp. Icicle-sharp.

Leaving the sparsely furnished reception area, Zolotov replayed his two-hour tête-à-tête with Dr. Philomena Rae. He'd set off a little after eight the previous evening. Figueroa had been conveniently indisposed – racked by pangs of guilt, she'd opted to press ahead with her research paper entitled 'The Trials and Tribulations of Emir Timur: the Ethnogenesis of Uzbekistan's National Hero'. His Porsche had roared past a hodgepodge of bookmakers, antique shops and tea houses on Burford's main shopping parade. Consulting his integrated GPS receiver, he'd followed the A361 as far as Cotswold Wildlife Park. Here, the Lechlade-bound road is joined by a quartet of tortuous country lanes. Zolotov had taken the third in the series. Swerving to avoid the remains of a flattened hedgehog, he'd cruised past some ivy-swaddled outbuildings. A farmhouse had materialised soon after.

With its exposed beams and quaintly angled walls, the smallholding might have been pilfered from a Slavic folktale. Having introduced himself as a 'one-time tutee of Judith's', Zolotov had followed his hostess down an unlit corridor. The scent of home-baked soda bread issued from a basement kitchen, sour yet delectable. His gaze drifted to a triangular wine-rack beneath the stairs. Of its seventy or so bottles, some three-fifths were non-vintage *Moët et Chandon Brut Impérial.* Several clarets, including his own beloved *Château Haut-Brion*, graced its lowermost shelves. A thick steel plinth ensured that none of Rae's downwardly-angled bottles came into contact with her laminate flooring.

In the stark light of the lounge, Zolotov began to scrutinise this most unlikely of Oxford dons. Rae was squat and ruddy-cheeked. Her tasseled loafers and chequered A-line skirt were an object lesson in the art of emphasising one's defects to the point that they virtually ceased to exist – at least in her eyes. Zolotov couldn't help but wonder just how far the economist adhered to this principle. Her blouse was made of worsted yarn, crew-necked and with sleeves buttoned to elbow level. She eyed him frigidly through her black fringe, an unwomanly hardness stamped upon her features. He put her at anything between forty-five and fifty-five. Never easy with such types, he reflected as she gestured him to a low-slung armchair by the French windows. A wood fire crackled in the hearth, imbuing the air with a sweet, fruity aroma.

Rae was not a wellspring of sorrow on learning that her friend and colleague had been found dead in bed. Far from it. Struggling to summon the customary expressions of sadness, she contented herself with a blend of incredulity and self-censoring gloom. Their conversation moved to the finer points of Saturday evening: the hearty meal; Olsten's theory about Olembé's true motives; the heated discussion on all things metaphysical; Olsten's uncharacteristic admission that life had been burdensome recently. Redford was mentioned, as was her predicament prior to the Dame's intervention.

'I, for my part, was never keen on this – the idea that Judith should fritter away her disposable income on Imogen. All those rental payments! Aye, the young are *always* better served by being left to fend for themselves. Natural selection . . . the sculptor of character.' She pursed her lips repressively. 'But it isn't for me to knock her judgement. Everything Judith did, she did sincerely and above board. Do you follow?'

'Naturally,' rebounded Zolotov. 'It sounds as if you knew her for a great many years, no? Tell me: what in Judith's past, remote or recent, might have precipitated death threats?'

Rae sat up jerkily. 'I'd no idea she'd been receiving *those*! Not like her to keep things hush-hush. Or perhaps it was a case of 'the more I feel, the less I show.'

'Feel what?'

'I really couldn't say,' she twittered, an eerie echo of her Tresingham superior. 'I imagine Judith was chilled to the core by the thought that someone should find her so objectionable. One of her own flock, perhaps.'

'That's not what I asked,' gnarled Zolotov. 'And she wasn't chilled to the core. Your college Master said so.'

'You've spoken to Reuben?'

'The very same.'

'Don't suppose he broached the subject of our ex-Master?'

Zolotov shook his head.

'Eugene Flanagan – that was the bampot's name – sported the mantle for the greater part of twenty years. A mild-mannered fellow who enjoyed the company of thirteen-year-old girls until he was so crudely unmasked. You *must* have read about it.'

'Can't say that I have,' confessed the Russian. 'You're not condoning his behaviour, are you?'

'Certainly not!' nipped Rae defensively. 'He disgraced the college in a way that Reuben Gershman would *never* do. Aye, perhaps his marital bonds were fracturing. Perhaps the ravages of time dampened his wife's affection. Perhaps the affection was there but not the urge.' Her features softened suddenly. 'Consciously or not, Flanagan wanted to regain control. In a final fling before his libido hit the skids, he sought out noncommittal intimacy where it could readily be had. A goal-driven junket. You'll agree that we *all* have our secrets,' she added without a flicker of fear. 'Our recesses of the soul, our double lives, our double-edged swords. I speak only figuratively, you understand.'

Zolotov rose from his armchair. Why only 'double'? he enquired of himself. Need there always be a limit? Why speak of Man's duality when he, for one, was many-sided – a garb for every occasion, every audience, every whim? Still steeped in Pirandello – his front-row seat at the Oxford Playhouse had been most agreeable – he was alert to a blurring of the theatre-reality frontier. Theatre, as 'The Father' had implied in Act III, was no less a part of life than sleep, food and defecation. The self was an anthology of different roles, a seedcoat sequestering the psyche, forever masking its nature.

He was sure that the transgressions of former Masters had little bearing on the investigation. Rather, it was Rae's blasé attitude to exploitative unions that merited attention. Anyone capable of explaining away something so abhorrent, so indelibly scarring to victim and family alike, was quite capable of anything. Adept at deceiving themselves. Adept at manipulating others.

'So what brings you here, then?'

The question came like a tongue from a salamander's mouth. There was something infra-human in that flattened face; those small, obliquely set eyes. The smugness in her voice unsettled him: she knew too much.

'I thought I'd answered that already. I'm a one-time tutee of Judith's and . . .'

'Yes, yes, but what *drives* you?' prodded the Glaswegian, rapping him teasingly across the knuckles. 'Intellectual curiosity? An undue interest in the peccancies of Oxford life? Voyeurism?'

As if on impulse, Zolotov's arms fell stiffly to his sides.

'For almost a decade, I was a voice in the wilderness, or as Fyodor Dostoevsky would have it, a plea from beneath the floorboards. Informers lurked behind every wall, every handset, every smile. When I ventured west from Irkutsk to Leningrad, the essence of fear was distilled, not diluted. Artificial buoyancy imposed a fiction on thought. I knew not what I knew not. Unknown unknowns. Years of censorship might have reduced my intellect to that of an automaton were it not for tortured souls – minor heroes! — who spoke their truths proudly and gallantly. I interviewed dozens: academics, Crimean Tartars, Jewish refuseniks. I did so in fear of my life, for how was I to know they were not KGB plants or paid informers? Defiance, risk – they run in my blood. Cossack blood. Not once did I consider becoming a fawning penman for *Pravda*, or a junior editor at the State Committee for Publishing. The reason, I presume, is obvious.'

Lowering his voice, Zolotov took three very deliberate steps towards the bemused don, the corners of his mouth curling downwards, then sideways.

'Here, I am buffered by the very academic tenure system that Judith took for granted. Like a high-ranking judge with a lifelong office, I am free to test received wisdom; to stray from safe lines of enquiry; to address unfashionable topics; to propose pioneering schema...or is it schemata? All without external pressure. I ask myself: why should this not apply to *all* facets of life?' He trained his stare on a stray hair thrusting its way through her brown tights. 'Twenty-seven years after defecting to this comparative haven of freedom, I have no plans to reapply the muzzle. Not now. Not ever. You'd do well to aid me in my endeavours.'

A queasy silence, broken only by the murmurings from the hearth. Rae studied him with unwholesome interest, as a palaeontologist might a fossilised moth. The faint lines flanking her snub nose began to deepen.

'You know what *your* problem is?' she uttered at last. 'You're completely mad wi' it!'

Intoxicated, Zolotov could only presume. High as a kite, in his cups, half-seas-over. Later that evening, he ran a phrase search on Google. An article entitled 'Glasgow Patter Goes South' confirmed that he was not far wrong.

The same couldn't be said for the Scot.

CHAPTER TWELVE

'In that carpeted matrix of tinted glass, computer stations and rolling aisles, he would sink probes into unfamiliar ground. Until then, all else was secondary.'

Zolotov's walk from Summertown to Oxford's bustling hub took just fifteen minutes. In the oily grey light, the Martyrs' Memorial looked even more forbidding than usual. At Magdalen Street's intersection with George Street, he took a minor detour: Boots. Having scoured the innermost aisles, he emerged with a plastic bag containing the last remaining blood pressure monitor. Widening his stride, he doubled back as far as Ship Street, powered past *The King's Arms* some three minutes later, and bore northeast as far as Manor Road.

The Manor Road Building housed the Social Science Library. Zolotov often wondered whether the panels embosoming the three-storey edifice were off-white, cream, or simply white. On this occasion, however, the question would remain academic. In that carpeted matrix of tinted glass, computer stations and rolling aisles, he would sink probes into unfamiliar ground. Until then, all else was secondary.

Beyond some revolving doors and a skylighted atrium, he swiped his Bod card through an electronic gate. At the nearby issue desk sat a weasel-eyed librarian by the name of Elspeth O'Carolan – or so her name badge proclaimed. With no attempt at diffidence, Zolotov introduced himself as 'the incumbent REES Professor'. From the zip pocket of his flannel trousers he withdrew a wallet, no longer bearing the laminated headshot of Anastasiya Zolotova, née Gushchina. Thumbing through his credit cards – rather too long for Miss O'Carolan's liking – Zolotov extracted a white OULS card.

'Top up the credit,' he decreed, handing her three two-pound coins. 'I have what you might call a tryst with the photocopier, no?'

The librarian duly processed his request, her quarter-smile suggesting that she found his behaviour more embittering than mirthful. Ruffling her frizzy hair, the girl now endeavoured to goad him into an ice-thawing exchange.

'If you *did* need the rolling aisles for statistical material,' she tattled in her heavy brogue, 'be sure to call for help with the gearing mechanism. Wouldn't want you getting squashed between the bookcases, now, would we?' she supplied, her voice curiously devoid of irony.

'Indeed we wouldn't,' he intoned on the half-turn.

Zolotov, as it happened, had scant interest in the rollstack treatises. Instead, he wended his way past three reshelving areas, before turning into an aisle tenanted only by journals. His attention was seized by the words 'Medical' and 'Law'.

Pausing to brush away a patina of dust from its exposed edges, he picked up a matt grey periodical. Boots bag tucked snugly under his shoulder, he ambled past some open-plan seating areas and into a glass-screened study room.

Zolotov liked the East Graduate Room. A potted cactus provided the sole imprint of nature in an otherwise clinical milieu. Furnished with plush chairs and height-adjustable worktops, it kept him away from the 'detritus that thinks itself savvy'. It was his sanctum; his home from home. More often than not, it was completely empty.

He pored over *The New England Journal of Applied Medical Law* until his neck ached. In an article spanning two dozen pages, Professor T. Roster of the American Constitution Society for Law and Policy argued that the justice system, civil and criminal alike, needed immediate 'rebalancing' in favour of the law-abiding majority; that '21st century offences required 21st century solutions'. Echoes of the UK Home Office, perhaps? Zolotov pictured the celebrated scales of Blind Justice, diligently weighing the evidence of the prosecution against that of the defence. Reading between the lines, Professor Roster was referring to an inherent need to expedite the conviction process by lowering the burden of proof. A lower burden of proof would mean an increase in the total number of convictions. Fewer wrongdoers would be acquitted, more innocent people convicted, casualties of a faster, meaner, more streamlined judiciary. Unless fresh evidence was brought to light, Zolotov reasoned, the outlook for Olembé was bleaker than ever. Delia was the *prima facie* victim, *his* victim, and so it was in her favour that any judgement would be weighted. The law, after all, was less about truth than about what could readily be proved. And still the question remained: was Olembé deserving of such a verdict?

Catching the officious eye of Miss O'Carolan as she boated past with a pile of books, he thought of the others who'd been laid low by the Olembé affair. They were a sundry bunch: Delia's relatives, bereaved of their loved one, hit hard by their failure to secure life insurance; Brett 'BramTech' Milligan, deprived of an enticing and potentially profitable business venture; Professor Trent, so close to cashing in on the Aussie's buyout offer; Olembé's insurers, riled at finding themselves on the brink of a mammoth payout.

One blast. Multiple shock waves.

Finding the air-conditioning somewhat overpowering, Zolotov decided to curtail his reading session. Journal in hand, he strolled over to the nearby photocopying suite, its quintet of Xerox copiers deep in sleep mode. Grinding his teeth in concentration, he inserted his OULS card into the digital reader. £8.40 remaining. With customary precision, he laid the journal on the glass platen, aligning it with both pairs of guide marks. He ran off his first double-page. Realigning the journal, he repeated this ritual no fewer than eleven times.

*

One more stop. Then a lightening of the load. Passing the stuccoed Indian Institute building, a tiny elephant crowning its gilded weathervane, Zolotov rejoined the kaleidoscope of central Oxford.

An open-top Tour Guides bus was berthed at the entrance to Catte Street. From it emerged a straggling column of Israeli tourists, led by a guide in an indigo cagoule. Some carried mewling infants, others buttressed aging relatives, the women abiding stringently by the Tzeniut code of modesty. A well-hewn girl caught his eye. Had she been alone, Zolotov might have been tempted to establish the frontiers of Talmudic levity by giving her a puckish wink, then gauging her reaction. Instead, in the inopportune presence of her two male companions, he threaded his way through a crush of iPhone-wielding sightseers, past the 'Bridge of Sighs', and onto the grey cobblestones of Radcliffe Square.

Marooned in an ocean of grass, the Radcliffe Camera was festooned with scaffolding. He knew it to be an integral part of the Old Bodleian Library, connected to its newer counterpart by a catacomb of underground rooms. 600,000 volumes below the rotunda alone, with a further 10,500,000 occupying some 120 miles of shelving university-wide. Not that his forage would take him anywhere near Oxford's bookstacks.

With the shuffling bodies receding, Zolotov began to climb the Rad Cam's dozen or so weathered steps, now as familiar to him as the ground on which he stood. Not for the first time, he had the impression of entering some huge, petrified wedding cake, three-tiered on the outside, two-storied on the inside. Gone were those heady days when he, a mere student, would approach locals with the question: 'Tell to me fastest route to University?' Or a wholly unanswerable: 'What time does Tesco 24 close?' Or an equally unavailing: 'Where can I find Dr. [insert surname] of history division, please?' How naïve he'd been to assume that those who did not know their 'bedels' from their 'battels', their 'bonners' from their 'bumpers', could be relied upon to direct a student they'd never met to a tutor they'd no intention of meeting? But 'Konny' had learned fast; so fast, in fact, that the person he once was would have struggled to recognise the person that life – that Oxford – that freedom – had made him.

The University Church was chiming out the hour as Zolotov withdrew his Bod card and flashed it with raptorial relish. He presented his Boots bag to a glum peroxide blonde in a grey uniform, seated as usual at a high wooden table opposite the entrance. Throwing him the disdainful look of an overburdened notary – or a ticket officer aboard the Trans-Siberian Express – the woman soon disabused herself of the idea that his blood pressure monitor was an Al-Qaeda-endorsed incendiary device. For this he was most grateful. With a brusque nod and a clink of glass beads, she bid him pass.

The Upper Camera Reading Room was suitably subdued, a hush broken only by the whispers of librarians and the shuffle of photocopiers. A dry, papery realm of dust, the air stagnant, baleful, expectant. Away to his right, a bevy of students were communing with their faintly humming laptops. Some were revising for Trinity term Collections, others refining dissertations ready for submission to the Research Degree Examination Office. Their assiduity both impressed and unsettled him – Easter Vac squandered, he too faced a familiar descent into the inferno that was, and would remain, Trinity term.

An islet of PCs brightened the sombre interior. Each terminal was a portal to OLIS, Oxford's library catalogue. Massaging his right temple, Zolotov breezed past the enquiry desk. Telnet was active, its DOS-like interface amounting to blocks of white text swamped by deepest black. How about a Subject Keyword search? Yes, that might work. He processed the possibilities: ancient Rome; imperial Rome; Roman history; writings from ancient Rome; Roman Emperors; tyranny in imperial Rome. 'Tyranny' yielded several hundred hits, the seventieth being Tacitus' *Annals of Imperial Rome.*

Gaius Cornelius Tacitus.

Zolotov had certainly heard of the biographer-cum-historian, but struggled to assign him a context; a canvas; a hook. Not that it bothered him in the slightest – that was where Google entered the fray. There were only two copies university-wide: one in Murgatroyd College (E 122.1 TAC), due back on the 08/05/10, the second in the Rad Cam's open-shelf history collection (T. HIST.11.40.21).

A solitary spiral staircase led to the gallery. It whorled like some oversized vine tendril, set free from the rotunda's Palladian regularity. With this image very much in mind,

Zolotov climbed its seventeen narrow stairs, balustrades trembling. He looked left, then right, then left again. Three-metre-high bookcases punctuated the arched walkway. Leather volumes stood beside cloth-bound ones, the dye faded on their fragile spines. His neck hairs bristled. Guided by the spine-affixed shelfmarks and a dose of intuition, he located the book in question. Penguin Classics, the 1956 edition. He settled down opposite a burqa-clad girl, her laptop drawing electricity from a nearby socket. The old and the new – an effortless fusion. After twenty minutes of feverish thumbing, he struck gold: a single passage, ten lines long. He withdrew his Sony Ericsson and removed its protective lens cover. Aligning the page with the 3.2 megapixel camera, he heard a series of clicks. Nine snapshots, four of them blurred. He stood to leave, open book in hand. Its pages fluttered as a rare draught blew across the gallery. His cotton voile shirt was damp against his back, uncomfortably tight as he straightened his spine.

Zolotov knew but two kinds of perspiration: warm from exertion; cold with fear.

This was neither.

CHAPTER THIRTEEN

'An intoxicating miasma engulfed the lounge: a mustiness akin to a damp wine cellar; subtle accents of vanilla; a candied tang of decadence.'

'Your poison, Dr. Olembé?'

'Er, sparkling water please. Feeling a bit woozy tonight.'

Earlier that evening, an unlikely sixsome had been summoned to St Aldates police station. Seven had appeared. They'd been greeted by an inscrutable Dárdai, formally identified and led aboard a fifteen-seater Ford Transit minibus. Five officers and Dr. Popham ensured parity. Their ride to Summertown had taken just eight minutes, the silence broken only by Gershman's lisped protests at having been 'supremely inconvenienced'. A miscellany of faces had appeared in Zolotov's peephole. Most were familiar to him; a few were not. With his guests seated, he'd proceeded to unlock his liqueur cabinet, its polychromatic bottles forming a jagged skyline against the glass.

'Some aqua vitae, Dr. Rae?'

'A wee dram of Lagavulin,' she chirped back. 'And no ice.'

Zolotov was primed for that one. 'My dear woman!' he

cried in mock exasperation, lilt more pronounced than ever. 'Who on *earth* do you take me for? Ice with vintage single malt, in flagrant disregard of its phenolic and peaty overtones? Flagitious cryogenic abuse!' Swaying theatrically, he reached for the next best thing: a cylindrical case of fifteen-year-old Laphroaig.

By quarter past nine, all but Dárdai and his Thames Valley contingent had been duly, if belatedly, served. From his vantage point beside a chrome uplight – Zolotov didn't 'do' lampshades – Dárdai cast an eye over the garish form of Salomea Gershman. Clad in a fuchsia dress, her gold fleck contact lenses distorted the objective reality of her eyes, lending them an almost phantasmal appearance. Why had she accompanied her husband in his professional capacity?

'Oh, how stunningly gaudy!' she squawked through the hushed pleasantries. 'I'm sure you'll agree, Doctor,' turning to a mortified Olembé, 'that each and every one of us has a dark side. Introverts, socialites, you name it: the blacker the berry, the sweeter the fruit.' Though greeted by a wall of silence, she babbled on regardless. 'For the promise of high drama, I need merely sit, watch and titter away at the spectacle as it unfolds. Smile, Doctor. Smile!'

A lit *Upmann Magnum 50* rollicked through her groomed digits, its dropped cinders speckling an ever broader tract of carpet. Hypoallergenic carpet. A vehement non-smoker since his defection, Zolotov gave the cigar-bearer a distasteful *coup d'œil* over the tops of his glasses. Then he began in earnest.

'Two deaths,' he droned. 'Two ill-fated, tragic deaths. Mr. Holdenby has lost a loving, and by all accounts heroic, wife. One who refused to capitulate in the face of impending ruin. Ruin from within.'

He glanced sympathetically in Holdenby's direction. The widower indicated concord with a sullen nod, his earlier swagger all but gone.

'In Dame Olsten,' resumed the Russian soulfully, 'though I never had the pleasure of meeting her, Tresingham College has lost a spirited and original thinker. One of the last of a pre-war generation still active in the academic crucible.' He paused to survey his spellbound audience. 'Two deaths, each with a straightforward explanation. A terminally ill cancer patient given false hope by a committed, if overzealous, virotherapy activist. One who placed undue emphasis on serendipity to the exclusion of skill – the skill of judgement. An aging professor found dead in her bedroom with an open pack of warfarin by her side. A tutor in receipt of death threats. A tutor with a diagnosed heart condition. What are we to infer? Accidental overdose? Suicide? Assisted suicide? Coincidental burnout?' He dabbed his perspiring brow with a blue cotton handkerchief. 'Two deaths, my friends. Two deaths.'

Shunning eye contact, the balding Dr. Popham sharpened his gaze on the electric feature fire. A warm glow emanated from its white pebble knoll, shifting figures dissolving into their alter-egos.

'Following a rigorous set of toxicology tests, I can confirm that high levels of warfarin were found in Delia H's bloodstream. That said, our post-mortem very nearly didn't happen. Only got there in the nick of time.'

Travis stuck up a fleshy, tremulous finger. 'Forgive me, but what exactly do you mean?'

'I mean we arrived at the funeral parlour minutes before our evidence was drained away and replaced with formaldehyde, as is standard practice. Allow me to guide you through my reasoning. Warfarin's relatively long half-life of thirty-six to forty-two hours means that several days are required for the drug to reach therapeutic effect; at least in standard doses. The biggest daily dose I've seen reported in the literature is two hundred milligrams. We now know, to a low probability of error, that Delia H was given two thousand, three hundred. The median lethal dose for warfarin in humans is estimated at between fifty and five hundred milligrams per kilogram of body weight, so if Delia H weighed forty-seven kilograms at the time of her death, it must follow that she was within the lethal range. As warfarin is metabolised by the liver and excreted by the kidneys, dosages must be lowered in patients with liver and kidney dysfunction. In her flagging state, her gross organ function would have been severely compromised, accentuating the effect of any warfarin. Bearing in mind that she was never a warfarin taker, we can discount the possibility of an accidental overdose. One should also note,' he added a trifle patronisingly, 'that when her body was originally checked for suspicious marks, the examiner found nothing; nothing but the customary pinhole left by the insertion of a peripheral IV catheter into one of her metacarpal veins during virotherapy. The only way to resolve our morass is as follows: someone with direct access to Delia H injected warfarin *over* the site of the virotherapy injection in a bid to avoid detection.' A wave of consternation swept across the room. 'Warfarin,' he continued edgily, 'is soluble both in water and in alcohol, so one can only presume that the killer used one of these solvents. The miniscule nature of our second pinhole, just 2.3 millimetres away from the first, convinced me of one thing: that a short-bevelled hypodermic needle was used to deliver the fatal dose.'

'And the syringe?' presented Dárdai.

'A plastic-barrelled, standard U-100 syringe was used. Their role in the daily ritual of diabetics explains their over-the-counter availability.'

'So no lingering doubts then, Popham?' The scornful edge to Dárdai's voice arose more from habit than wilful disdain.

'Virtually none. Now over to you . . . eh . . . Zolotov.'

The Russian spread his arms like a co-celebrant at an offertory. Nudges, whispers and winks traversed the lounge.

'My thanks, Doctor. You have dealt exhaustively with the how. I, meanwhile, shall devote my energies to the *who* . . . which instantly brings me to you, Mr. Holdenby. When I presented myself at your door, inveigling you with my aquamarine business card, your demeanour said it all. Crude, opportunistic ghostwriter locked horns with grieving husband. It was the former that won. Overwhelmingly so.'

The once doleful Holdenby had sprung to life at the first mention of his name. 'What are you implying?'

'If you listen to the wording, my friend, you'll realise that I've made no explicit accusations whatsoever. I might ask, hypothetically of course, whether it was you who killed your wife? If you *did*, I beg the question – why? If not, my question remains a valid one. To move us closer to an answer, I ask myself when, in her final days, was Delia's underbelly at its most exposed? When undergoing her first and last virotherapy session? During her forty-eight-hour quarantine at the Churchill? Or was it later on, dear people? Surely not at home, by which time Delia had regained her faculties quite sufficiently to sense the presence of an intruder. Unless,' he added darkly, 'our intruder was hidden from view.'

Rae fixed her eyes on his. 'Hidden? How do you mean, hidden?'

'I mean that our intruder was masquerading as a medic, friend or relative, no strings attached. Someone who'd secured the trust of Delia Holdenby. Someone intent on abusing it.'

Dárdai's lupine features contorted into a cringe. 'But that implicates at least *five* individuals, Zolotov, buying us a one-way ticket to nowhere.' Not for the first time that evening, he found himself bewailing Zolotov's fondness for hyperbole to the apparent exclusion of method.

'We shall see, János. Doctor Olembé – this whole investigation has been inordinately strenuous. Would you be so kind as to measure my blood pressure? Everything you require hails from Boots.'

On the chrome-rimmed coffee table, still sheathed in its airtight sachet, was a blood pressure monitor. Rather than the traditional 'bulb and gauge', Zolotov had acquired a digital unit with a trigger-release air valve. Puzzled, and more than a little self-conscious, Olembé looked to Dárdai for authorisation.

But Zolotov was indefatigable. 'Oh, I implore you, Doctor! Perhaps the old myocardium isn't quite as robust as it used to be,' he supplied, exchanging oblique glances with Figueroa, 'but what else can one expect from years of *Pyatizvyozdnaya* drip-feed, no?'

Still hesitant, Olembé instructed Zolotov to unclench his fist. Supporting his right arm at heart level, he fastened the Velcro strap and pressed 'Start'. The machine buzzed purposefully as the strap tightened.

'Fine,' said Olembé some ten seconds later. 'One-thirty over eighty-nine – for what it's worth.'

'And heart rate, Doctor. Just for the record.'

'Seventy-three beats per minute.'

'Splendid, splendid. Now your turn, Miss Redford. Please do the honours.'

Placing her brandy glass on a coaster, the unshapely woman rose charily from an armchair. One hand clutched the nape of her neck. 'Look, I'm not sure whether . . .'

'. . . you might run the risk of overburdening the air valve? Perish the thought. But do remind us, in your capacity as a qualified NMC health visitor, what name is given to the contraption used to measure blood pressure?'

Redford stared fixedly at the ceiling, as if holding back a tide of expletives. 'Now *what* did they call it at nursing school? Apparatus? Device? Gadget? Completely slipped my mind. Damn! Begins with a 'z', I think.'

'Sphygmomanometer,' rasped Zolotov, 'or 'sphyg' in nurse's jargon.' He unfastened the Velcro strap. 'Which, my friends, brings me to my next question: how is it that Mr. Holdenby came to place so much trust in the services of Miss Redford? In an earlier conversation, he alluded to what we now know to be an entirely fictitious advertisement in the *Oxford Journal*.'

'Fictitious?'

'You heard me, Redford. A few hours ago, at the behest of Superintendant Cleaver, DCI Dárdai called in on the tabloid's Managing Director at her Abingdon offices. She confirmed that none by the name of Imogen Redford had ever – I repeat, ever! – posted an NMC advertisement in the designated columns.' His eyes narrowed. 'As some of you may know, the Radcliffe Infirmary closed for medical use in January 2007. The Churchill and the JR have since shared the burden of the relocated facilities. But why do I mention this? Because Redford claimed to have worked at the Infirmary for the greater part of six years – that's what Holdenby told us. Dárdai's research suggests otherwise. On the database of ex-Infirmary staff, Imogen Redford is nowhere to be found. She *is*, however, in the employ of a local conveyancing firm, a part-time secretary earning under fifteen thousand per annum. So I tender the following question: was Holdenby tricked by Miss Redford, or was it what you English might call 'a shared whopper'?'

Zolotov lingered on the last consonant. In a flamboyant sweep, he turned his back on the assembled party. Craning his neck through a wide-flung window, he paused to register the sycamore's majestic boughs, the amber streetlights, the vistas of darkness, the blue and yellow Battenburg markings adorning the police minibus. He could have sworn he had caught snatches of the Clapperton Boating Song from Canterbury Road. Indeed he had. Its lyrics became steadily clearer, the tune to Lord of the Dance ever more recognisable:

Coxswain, whoever you may be
Not quite the cream of royalty
Shouldn't grouse
Could be Scouse
Chewing lice in a council house

And there it coalesced. On inhaling the resinous coating of the black chesspiece, Zolotov had detected more than ebony heartwood – the lingering base notes of a woody eau de toilette had been perceptible also. The conclusion was inescapable: hours, perhaps minutes, before his Porsche had steered into London Road, Holdenby had been challenging a certain lady to a spot of chess. The game had been cut short, the gardening undertaken. His chess partner had remained upstairs, silent as a mamba. 'Holdenby 2', as the ghostwriter had so nimbly embroidered it, was nothing but a smoke-screen. Hadn't he a soupçon of grace? Couldn't the consummation of his affair have waited for the first dusting of soil to descend upon Delia's coffin?

Without warning, Zolotov turned on a sixpence. 'My dear people,' he whispered, drawing a cacophony of laughter from Salomea Gershman. 'Our imposter, you'll find, is also our unlikely lover. A devotee of cedar and sandalwood, think you not?'

He cast his reptilian eyes about the room, inclining first towards Reverend Travis, then Rae, then Figueroa, then Olembé. They came to rest, unblinking, upon the sweater-clad figure of Miss Redford.

'What?' gasped Holdenby, now crimson with rage. 'How downright speculative!'

Zolotov gave an effusive jolt of surprise. 'Does it *really* strain credulity to snapping point? It's well known that the costs of malpractice litigation are exorbitant. Administrative expenses, not to mention the monstrous conditional fees charged by prosecuting lawyers, have been known to equal – yes *equal*! – the compensation paid to plaintiffs. In rare cases, the conditional fee may actually surpass the amount awarded in damages. Seen by some as a disgusting vehicle for retribution, these cases often result from a greater desire on the part of the wronged to flog the defending party than to recover damages. That's what Mr. Holdenby would have us believe when he resolved to "stop that incompetent quack in his tracks"; to discipline him "in respectful memory" of his wife. The emphasis was on punishment, never profit.'

Zolotov dropped his voice abruptly. 'Earlier today, I had the good fortune to skim *The New England Journal of Applied Medical Law*. And what do I learn? I learn that years, not months, separate the alleged misdeed from the closure of the malpractice claim. Professor Roster asserts that a third of claims his side of the Atlantic take six or more years to resolve. You, Mr. Holdenby, were quite prepared to wait, for if Delia's murder could be made to look like Olembé's negligence, compensation would have topped two million pounds. It was evil of the highest order, yet you stood to pocket a life-changing sum in emotional damages. Irony of ironies, no?'

'Tripe!' cried Holdenby. 'I'm rich enough as it is, dammit! Audi R8s don't grow on trees. Why in the blazes would I . . .'

But Zolotov lanced through him unabashedly. 'Earlier today, Dárdai secured authorisation to access your online bank account. As of Tuesday, 13th of April, 4.49 pm, you are overdrawn by a total of fourteen thousand, nine hundred pounds. Asset rich yet cash poor. RH Ltd, the one-man company in whose coffers you'd have me deposit many a five-figure cheque, finds itself on the brink of liquidation. We have our smoking gun.'

Removing his spectacles, Zolotov began to degrease his left lens with a black microfibre cloth.

'Isn't it farcical how unexacting technology can be in the standards demanded of its users? Their morals, their motives, their secret pasts? It has, like a licenced firearms dealer, the capacity to serve law-maker and law-breaker alike. Assuaging the troubles of some. Compounding those of others. But I digress,' he relented, presumably addressing his own tangential streak. 'Let us turn now to our second untimely demise. Four people in this room can claim to have known the late Dame Olsten. First, we have Dr. Rae,' to which the Glaswegian gave a cluck of irritation. 'We then have Miss Redford, followed swiftly by our inviolable man of the cloth. Bringing up the rear is the redoubtable Professor Gershman. I should add that Melissa Rawal was last seen gallivanting with her staunch chums in Cowley, no? Just for the record, I spent Monday evening in Burford, endeavouring to keep pace with the ebullient intellect of Dr. Rae. She gladly confirmed all the pranks and pratfalls of what would prove to be Olsten's last supper. Doctor – you tell me that Olsten supported Redford financially?'

'Aye. In return for . . .'

'And Redford accepted this gratefully and graciously?'

'Graciously?' spurted the Scot. 'Would have been more gracious to refuse, if you ask me.'

'It just so happens that I'm *not*, Doctor. But no matter. At one point last Saturday, you couldn't help noticing a change in Redford's demeanour, no?'

'A look of inexplicable alarm, verging on enmity. I suppose Judith and I were being a tad heavy in sandbagging some of her more sweeping assertions, if you'll permit, Imogen. Under normal circumstances, mind you, it would've been water off a duck's back.'

'Anecdotal evidence!' snarled Redford.

Dr. Rae flared her nostrils at her former tutee. 'Don't pee on my leg and tell me it's raining, Imogen. Something was wrong that evening. If Judith was alive now, bless her, she'd vouch for my account.'

'What, specifically, do you think Redford was reacting to, Doctor?'

'To Judith's suggestion of foul play. Infiltration by a rival pharmaceutical firm.'

'Ni'aha, the rival company! The company that botched the poisoning job so badly that Delia spent a full two days in a stable condition before being discharged? Yes indeed. But do continue, Doctor.'

'As I was within seconds of highlighting, Judith went on to suggest that a post-mortem would reveal all.'

'Reveal all, you say? At what point in the dinner was this?'

'Right before coffee. I'm sure of it.'

With a practised hand, Zolotov whipped out his PDA from an inner pocket. He cradled it tenderly in his waxen palms.

'I quote chapter thirteen, verse fourteen, of Gaius Cornelius Tacitus' magnum opus, *The Annals of Imperial Rome*.'

Holdenby was livid. 'Back to the primordial sludge, you crank! How in God's name is this relevant to . . .'

'Raconteurs hate to be interrupted, Mr. Holdenby. But I can assure you that we'll be arriving at platform N-M-I-S-W-K-N-W-T-B-I in under a minute.'

Of all the stares that greeted Zolotov, Dárdai's claimed

the laurels. If he were being charitable, he might contend that the Russian was gracing a loftier, abstruser intellectual plane; that there was method to his ostensible madness. By the same token, his old university friend might just have taken leave of his senses. Had the culprit come in the form of that savagely struck cricket ball, catching an unsuspecting Zolotov clean in the brow during an intercollegiate fixture at Port Meadow? A fortnight shy of twenty-eight, he'd claimed to find the concussive trauma 'refreshingly psychedelic, think you not?', as if cheerfully consulting a fellow pill-popper at a rave party. Nonplussed paramedics had promptly withdrawn his nitrous oxide supply as he lay delirious on an ambulance stretcher – for this was no laughing matter. Could it be that the delayed consequences of nodding off whilst fielding 'silly mid-on' were more pronounced than he cared to admit?

'Now listen carefully,' purled Zolotov, refocusing his attention on the backlit screen, 'for *here* is the passage in question: "It was the custom for young imperial princes to eat with other noblemen's children of the same age at a special, less luxurious table, before the eyes of their relations. That is where Britannicus dined. A selected servant habitually tasted his food and drink. But Nero thought of a way of leaving this custom intact without giving himself away by a double death. Britannicus was handed a harmless drink. The taster had tasted it; but Britannicus found it too hot and refused it. Then cold water containing the poison was added. Speechless, his whole body convulsed. He instantly ceased to breathe."'

'How utterly preposterous!' yawped Redford. '*Me*, lacing milk with warfarin . . .' She faltered to a halt, incensed by the folly of her own blunder.

'To douse the fires of Olsten's imaginings,' said Zolotov with aplomb. 'Misgivings you feared she'd divulge to the police. Theories you had to silence at all costs.'

'Yes, but . . . but she paid my rent. Why would I kill someone to whom I was so indebted?'

'Precisely the conclusion you wished us to draw, Miss Redford. You were nothing more than an outlet for the Dame's feelings of charity, ready to be discarded as unworthy of help the moment you stopped pandering to her self-importance. When you crossed that line so brazenly on Saturday evening, it was then that she became as expendable as feeble Delia. Olsten might well have forestalled your own eviction from Cotman Close, Miss Redford, but what if Holdenby were bolstered by a large Lorenex payoff? The promise of plusher quarters – *his* quarters – soon allayed your fears of dispossession. That three-way sparring match on the theories of ultimate meaning pressed home the vacuity of your own existence. By dispatching Olsten, you hoped to expunge all relics of a life of inglorious dependence; to supplant it with one of soirées, fast cars and designer clothing. When you needed her, you saved her life – as you did in Paris. When your needs changed, you murdered her.' He sapped Redford's feigned poise with a macabre, penetrating stare. 'You eat the same rollmops. You sip the same Lambrusco. Yet Dr. Rae is alive and well. As are you. Later that evening you drink the same coffee. Olsten brews it herself, but neglects to bring the milk. Rae told me this yesterday. You seize your moment. From the sanctuary of your kitchenette, you dissolve the flavourless warfarin in the milk you later bring to the table. An unwitting Olsten adds the milk to her mug of coffee. You add some to your *own* mug, for you always take it white. Naturally, you refrain from drinking it. Some seven hours after returning home to Jericho that night – a taxi ride she makes alone – Dame Olsten is dead, sealing her own fate with a bedtime dose of warfarin. Correct me if I'm wrong, Miss Redford.'

All vestiges of defiance crumbled with a piercing wail. 'Why goad me? Why torment me? That creaky old bitch was living on borrowed time. So was Delia. I took life so that I could live. Now, I have nothing! Richard has nothing!'

Olembé shook his head slowly. 'But why kill my patient? Why not simply wait . . . wait in hope that the treatment failed?'

'A legitimate enquiry,' returned Holdenby icily. 'There were, as Imogen and I saw it, four discrete scenarios. One: Delia would die *in spite* of virotherapy. Two: Delia would die *because* of virotherapy – an inbuilt risk all trialists take. Three: Delia would die due to gross medical negligence *following* virotherapy. Four: Delia would recover *thanks* to virotherapy. The last scenario could never be allowed to crystallise, so we manufactured the only lucrative one. Number three.'

In a strident blast, Dárdai made his belated entrance. 'A word of congratulations, Miss Redford. You covered your tracks so deviously that none of us thought of questioning you in the aftermath of either death. The first murder was quite ingenious. Having injected Delia with warfarin – and waited hours for it to take effect – you went through the rigmarole of calling the emergency services. By the time paramedics arrived to stem her haemorrhaging, her bell had long tolled. Any inferences made at the scene arose from the false assumption that her internal bleeding was a by-product of cancer.'

'Or a delayed response to virotherapy,' supplied Popham.

'Hence the absence of a full forensic post-mortem,' appended Zolotov. 'No inquest. No conviction.' The abhorrence in his cheeks thickened. 'And who in their right mind would suspect *you*, Mr. Holdenby? The man who seemed so intent on steering his wife through the medical works. Who left no stone unturned. Now we can only speculate on whether virotherapy held the key.'

*

Redford and Holdenby offered little resistance as they were escorted to Tanley Court's dim stairwell. Tailing them closely was János Dárdai, head hung low, ensnared in thought. But Figueroa noticed a curious spring in his otherwise metronomic step. The former she attributed to shame; the indignity of being so wide of the mark in believing that the case was 'all but wrapped up'. The latter she ascribed to unalloyed relief; delight at tying up the loose strands in a legalistic jumble. Rewarding when solved. Ruinous if mishandled.

'And the death threats?' demanded Gershman, stabbing his wife's spent cigar end into an ashtray. 'The safety of my staff may still be at risk.'

'Funny you should mention that,' mused Zolotov. 'You moved so fast with the Olsten affair, the sudden surge of air might have damaged you irreparably.' He tugged at his left earlobe for dramatic effect. 'And to think of the constabular legions that were summoned in her name; the internal investigations duly conducted; the manifold . . .'

'E-e-e-enough!' stammered Gershman. 'I was obliged to honour Olsten's request for confidentiality. You're not only rude, Zolotov, but pathologically arrogant.'

'And you, my friend, are rude for calling me arrogant, and arrogant for calling me rude. If her welfare meant so much to you, honour should have been consigned to the depths. Thanks to you, the machinations behind the death threats are, and may remain, a secret. One she will carry to the grave.'

*

Agape with revelation, the last of the party drifted apart like sparks from a fire. Three 001 Taxis had been ordered, the police minibus set aside for accomplice and killer. An intoxicating miasma engulfed the lounge: a mustiness akin to a damp wine cellar; subtle accents of vanilla; a candied tang of decadence.

The Cameroonian alighted from an armchair. 'Zolotov!' he warbled, thumping the Russian jovially on the back.

'You've salvaged more than my integrity – you've salvaged my sanity! And once this furore has simmered down, I've every chance of persuading fifty trialists that their coordinator isn't another Harold Shipman. Thanks to you, the only case I'm destined to encounter is a suitcase.'

Neuralgic twinges in Zolotov's back had impelled him into his swivel chair. 'Oh really?' he remarked dryly. 'Where are you off to?'

'Ulan Bator would be my preference. Never been beyond the stomping grounds of what my nephew calls 'Eurafrica'. And the Gandan Monastery, with its sixty-tonne statue of a Buddhist bodhisattva, is allegedly stunning.'

'As was your hospitality,' interjected Figueroa, silver bangles clinking. 'Extremely kind of you to serve up hand-crafted cocktails like that. Don't think me churlish, Doctor, but what came over you exactly?'

'Hum, good question,' rippled Olembé. 'From the way your outré colleague announced himself at my door, I assumed him to be one of those insufferable utopian socialists from *The Observer*. Nothing he said or did drove the idea from my mind.'

Zolotov sniffed the air. 'So you stopped short of bribery and resorted to tactical congeniality? Hoped we'd put in a good word for you?'

Olembé rolled his eyes. 'Something like that. Oh, and I meant to ask you,' he piped, breaking out into a rare smirk. 'What on earth is platform N-M-I-S-W . . .?'

'I thought you'd never ask,' grinned back Zolotov. 'That, Doctor, is a figurative platform. No trains.'

'Yes, but what does it *stand* for?'

'It stands for "No Man Is Sane Who Knows Not When To Be Insane". Strangely topical, think you not?'

CHAPTER FOURTEEN

'For reasons soon to become apparent, he dashed the flute from her coral lips with a deft swipe of the hand.'

Trinity term beckoned. Church spire and college turret exuded films of warmth from their pockmarked exteriors. With summer pervading the air, voracious swallows arrowed from the eaves. Wreathed with creepers, each shimmering wall wallowed in a veil of pride. Once an inane flouting of the rules, mischief became a compulsion, impelling the drunken student to stand at the precipice of Magdalen Bridge and crown their May Morning with a brainless belly-flop into the murky waters of the River Cherwell; or transform artful punting into a ramming war; or exploit the not so novel concept of post-exam celebrations: for some, a chance to mark the arrival of vacations with Pimm's and champagne; for others, a pretext to hurl buckets of pig's trotters, *crème fraîche* and turkey giblets – fresh and flexuous from the Covered Market – at their gown-clad chums. 'Each to his own' was never more apt than in the backstreets of Examination Schools.

While Zolotov surveyed these scenes with lofty detachment, the more creative shenanigans struck a chord with him. Famously or infamously, dependent entirely on the allegiances of those interrogated, 'Konny' had been the unheralded mastermind of a 1985 scheme to embellish the Murgatroyd College fountain. It had been *his* idea to call in on a local joke shop, to purchase an inflatable nude bust of Dolly Parton, and – ill met by moonlight – to smuggle it through the main quadrangle, a second gateway, and into the Fellows' Quad. Spurred on by a couple of aides, he'd proceeded to lever the bust – exhibiting the yellow and blue scarf of Clapperton College – to the tallest of three basins. All in vengeance for Clapperton's trouncing at the hands of its fiercest rowing rivals. All in time for the sunrise constitutional of Murgatroyd's unsuspecting Master.

*

Lying in wait was an eight-week marathon – nine-week if 'noughth' week was included in the reckoning. A seasoned member of the REES hierarchy, Zolotov braced himself for another departmental reshuffle. By the start of the Long Vacation he would have overseen the promotion of three Junior Research Fellows to the rank of lecturer, the appointment of an external candidate to the vacant readership, and the retirement of a Russian language instructor on grounds of ill-health. Simple.

Figueroa, meanwhile, prepared to summon that acute

blend of flexibility and organisational rigour demanded by her seniors. Assisting Zolotov would now consist chiefly of peer review and article submission for the monthly edition of REES Journal. Each assignment would be superimposed on her usual weekly classes with a dozen or so undergraduates. All too aware that the rewards for enterprising tuition seldom rivalled those for research, Figueroa gravitated towards the latter whenever the two came to blows.

Mindful of her looming drudgery, Zolotov scheduled a meeting devoted to a 'gravimetric appraisal of recent events, no?' That, at least, was how he cloaked it in a florid email, set to nothing less than High Priority. After much deliberation, he settled on Trás-os-Montes, a Brazilian-owned cocktail bar adjoining the Old Bank Hotel. He greeted her at its glass frontage a little after six-thirty. The dying light, punctuated by a few errant rays of sun, enhanced the olive tones of her blemishless complexion. To his pleasant surprise, she'd opted for Lucite stilettos and a strapless sequin dress. Onyx-black. Fitting, perhaps, for a wild Saturday shindig. Yet he stood in the balmy heat of an unspectacular Tuesday, blazer and polo-neck, the hour barely passable as evening.

'E aí, tudo bem?' flexed Zolotov, sauntering in after her. But his question was directed at the ponytailed proprietor behind the bar. Hearing a familiar voice, the man ceased polishing his Collins glass and smiled a roguish 'I see you're not alone this time'. Zolotov merely shrugged. Climbing the helical staircase, he selected a table near the mezzanine's edge. Barely had he finished helping Figueroa to her fibreglass chair when they were approached by a swarthy waiter.

'The usual, sir?'

'Not today, Luiz,' replied Zolotov inertly. 'Bring us two Russians: white for her, black for me. No cherries. No chocolate sticks.'

It was then that Figueroa's eyes slewed towards the leather briefcase tucked awkwardly under her supervisor's shoulder. Bulky and double-gusseted, it was ludicrously incompatible with his diminutive figure. Was this the vector for yet more departmental paperwork? Had he reneged on his promise of an informal drink? Her fears were allayed when Zolotov handed a bubble-wrapped champagne bottle to the bystanding waiter. 'Geladeira, vinte minutos!' – his barked instructions. But before she could respond accordingly, he'd whipped off his glasses, rubbed his eyes, and begun to verbalise in the lilting drawl that was his trademark.

'Down at her Burford smallholding, Dr. Rae gave me a sketch account of her ex-tutee's medical history. Redford, as I garnered from the Scot, had been unfortunate enough to develop deep vein thrombosis back in late 2009. This followed a freak injury during a badminton match at Iffley Road Sports Centre. The ankle fracture was innocuous enough, but a distinct lack of physiotherapy and a constricted cast precipitated the inevitable. While she was at it, Rae spoke of Olsten's even more serious brush with thrombosis, mentioning Redford's kindly hospital visits while the Dame was incapacitated by the condition in

Paris. Remember, Rena, that it was Olsten's propensity for blood clots that triggered her heart attack in the first place. Redford's visits, I later gathered, were kindly only in name, for she was merely laying the groundwork for a reciprocation of goodwill.'

'So?' pressed Figueroa, eyes widening.

'So Redford knew of Olsten's reliance on warfarin. She knew how the drug worked and was prepared to use that knowledge for her own ends.'

'But why set so much store by what Dr. Rae said? How do you know *she* was telling the truth, huh?'

'Other than her lack of a motive for concealment or murder, I didn't. But last week's events seem to vindicate my judgement, think you not?'

'Well, then – thank goodness for Tacitus.'

'Thank goodness for Zolotov's encyclopaedic knowledge of Roman history,' sniggered the Russian, stroking his cleft chin. 'Had the more learned members of our jamboree asked me a single supplementary question on Cornelius Tacitus, anything over and above what I'd saved on my PDA, I would have been screwed! Completely and unconditionally screwed! My knowledge of that era is about as broad as a Borzoi's snout.'

'But suppose Redford had kept her mouth shut?'

'Lucky dip,' chuckled Zolotov. 'Just like my Porsche. But even if she hadn't fallen for my ruse and confessed, forensic markers on those U-100 syringes might still have linked her to the first crime.'

'But what if Redford disposed of . . .'

'Then my hypothesis might still be confirmed by contacting the registrar at her warfarin clinic.' His eyes twinkled. 'After all, both murders were the result of Redford using warfarin from her *own* collection, no?'

Figueroa nodded, somewhat falteringly.

'So Redford would have been desperately short of warfarin after the murder of Delia Holdenby. You don't have to be a genius to work out what Redford did next.'

'Let me guess,' offered Figueroa. 'She phones her local anticoagulation clinic, explains that she's misplaced several blister packs, expresses concern at having interrupted the course, drops the idea that she's an experienced nurse, and insists on a repeat prescription. Surprise, surprise – more warfarin!'

Zolotov discharged a gravelly laugh. 'Good to know your time with me hasn't been *entirely* bootless. Which brings me to some important news. Earlier today, I mobiled DCI Dárdai. Apart from asking me to convey his regards to you – a phenomenon as rare as red rain – he revealed that forensics were busy doing what they do best: combing houses.'

'London Road and Cotman Close?'

'Precisely.'

'But why? The confessions are in the bag!'

'A logical objection, Rena. But from what Dárdai said, Superintendent Cleaver wanted to mop up a few outstanding issues, not least the origin of those death threats. So far, it's as I expected: not a single piece of forensic evidence linking Redford to the razor blades.'

'So who *did* write the note?'

'Hazarding a guess, I'd say it was the work of a highly disgruntled postgraduate – the only group Olsten supervised in her final years. The motive? Anything ranging from an acute personality clash, to the misguided impression that Olsten was showing favouritism in, say, the *viva voce*. Your guess is as good as mine.'

'Sounds credible, I suppose.'

'And therein lies its brilliance, Rena. In its plausibility.'

For the first time that week, words failed the Argentine. Her stare was like time itself, reducing Zolotov to nothing, prying at his guilt. Then she spurted: 'You don't mean . . . you don't *honestly* mean you played some part in its arrival at Tresingham?'

'Some part, Rena? I wrote it! First, I procured an adhesive envelope to avoid depositing saliva on the flap. I wore latex gloves when transferring the Lucida typeface from an overlaid piece of tracing paper onto my blank sheet. Simple. Leather gloves were donned for stage three: delivery to Olsten's pigeonhole. Why did Gershman accept my flimsy explanation about student frolics so unquestioningly? Because it offered a sense of order within chaos.'

Figueroa shifted furiously in her chair. '¡Dios mío! Don't you regret it?'

'Not bitterly, Rena. What I regret – and make no mistake about it – is that Olsten's final days were not as pleasant as they might have been. She didn't purchase a burglar alarm for nothing . . . and the razor blades *were* in rather poor taste. But before you become as stroppy as a mallard duck, allow me to address the reason. It's true: I never *did* cross paths with that stifled sapphist. Not directly. Yet my Shcherbatov research paper, destined for the *British Journal for the History of Philosophy*, adheres to her like a pin to a magnet.' Zolotov glanced at the miniature glitter ball rotating steadily above them. 'There is,' he resumed, 'the small but genuine possibility that I left draft C in the History Faculty Library. Stranger things have happened. We know she frequented the HFL because Dárdai spotted the library stamp in her copy of *Democracy in America*.'

'And so you punish her for your mistake?'

'*She* made the mistake, Rena. Seems her interest in Russia did not stop at Aleksandr Borodin and his orchestral works, but spilled over into Prince Mikhailo Shcherbatov and the Russian Enlightenment. Part philosopher, part ideologue, his view of human nature and social progress is kindred to Swift's satirical pessimism. But I digress. Olsten was a smooth and canny operator. She knew that once my article was safely through the peer review process – based, in the *BJHP*'s case, on initial editor screening and anonymous refereeing – she would be met with a vicious publisher backlash. Not worth the risk. But what if the article could be purloined before the assignment of copyright? A very different story.'

Figueroa pierced the momentary lull. 'Strange that a proven academic should resort to this, huh?'

'Not if 'publish-or-perish' came into play.'

She blinked at him, puzzled.

'You disappoint me, Rena. 'P-or-P', as I like to call it, refers to a pressure you are already familiar with: the need for frequent publication in order to sustain one's career in academia; to ensure a steady stream of research funding.'

'But how does it apply to the Dame?'

'Isn't it obvious? Gershman told us that Olsten had missed out on a remunerative professorial chair, so we can safely presume that her retirement package was modest at best. When she applied for an Emeritus professorship at the turn of the millennium, she knew she would be working under a specific set of University rules. A non-tenured position. Inherent uncertainty. With so much of her monthly outlay going on Redford, publish-or-perish became especially germane.' He made an unlikely church steeple of his fingers. 'I've subscribed to that journal for well over a year now. As I browsed through the February issue, my reworked article popped out at me like a jack-in-the-box. Its words, its nodes of energy, tormented me with their thwarted promise. *My* words. *My* promise. To do nothing would have been scholastic martyrdom. Unlike some, I had no wish to emulate Christ by discarding the self, only to recover it in heavenly life.' Not coincidentally, the Russian's steeple collapsed. 'I may have mentioned,' he continued, 'that Dárdai found several preprints in Olsten's fireproof safe – D, E and F, as well as the final version. But drafts A, B and C were nowhere to be found.'

'Oh?'

His voice wavered, then broke. 'Because they were *mine*! Mine and mine alone. D was made with the help of C –

the one that I misplaced – with C subsequently destroyed. One presumes that the token changes between D, E and F were intended to convey an impression of steady refinement in the event of a search. Where was her *amour propre*? Her intellectual pride? No wonder she asked Gershman to hush the matter up! If the reason for those death threats ever surfaced, her name would be elk dung. Ah! Our Russians draw near.' Zolotov politely acknowledged the arrival of the cocktails, but swiftly resumed his impassioned account. 'In answer to Rae's question – "so what drives you?" – I ended up telling her everything.'

'Everything?'

'Well, almost everything. How I was betrayed by the very motherland I'd been reared to cherish. How I defected to Britain to unshackle myself from faceless oppression. You forget, Rena, that my tutor at Leningrad State University was committed to a rural *psikhushka*, a nuthouse, for his alleged contact with foreign journalists.'

'Which nuthouse?'

'Litvinov Psychiatric Hospital No.1, a hundred miles north of Moscow. For three degrading hours, he was forced to adopt a foetal position while a doctor repeatedly inserted a nine-centimetre needle into his spinal canal. No local anaesthetic was used, no cerebrospinal fluid ever collected for future analysis – not that analysis was the point of the exercise. This excruciating ritual continued for over six months, the damage to his nervous system irreversible. But the "politically defined madness" was adjudged to have gone. Against this backcloth of persecution, of rampant human rights abuse, who can blame me for being protective of my new niche? Of reacting instinctively when Olsten threatened my academic autonomy in a way far darker, more Machiavellian, than anything I encountered back home? The lowest depth to which a soul can sink. Yes, I sought to reclaim control by way of a crank note; threats I had no intention of carrying out. You must understand, Rena, that when I wrote "your days are numbered", my words were couched as a harmless reminder that advancing senility and dubious judgement do not sit easily with the rigours of professorship. A dangerous precedent. By "days", I was referring to her time as an Oxonian, not as a *Homo sapiens*.'

As Zolotov shut his eyes with stung pride, Figueroa considered the ramifications of this disclosure. Then her eyes lit up.

'You mean our Tresingham trip was a complete waste of time? A two-hour water-muddier?'

'In some senses, yes,' Zolotov returned flatly. 'It told us little about the murderer or her motives.' He sipped his cocktail. 'Having said that, we owe our clinching testimony to Gershman – it was he who gave us Rae's name. Why did I pursue the Olsten case so avidly? To reassure myself that my threats hadn't driven her to suicide; that her death was by another's hand. If there were confessions to extract, it was my duty to extract them. And one more thing,' he added in a conspiratorial whisper. 'On no account must Dárdai hear of this.'

'And what are the chances of *that*?'

'Low-to-negligible if you keep your mouth shut. Fortunately for me, the pixel resolution of the Tresingham cameras precludes recordings of forensic quality. Same system as Clapperton's. And even if Big Brother *did* catch me entering the porter's lodge on that blustery afternoon in March, it would have missed me depositing the envelope in Olsten's pigeonhole. Out of range, no?'

'So why worry?'

'Because with Trinity term approaching, the Olsten case will be roused from its temporary slumber. Tresophytes will return from their holidays armed with a glut of questions.'

'*Must* you answer them?'

'I don't plan to; but you can be sure the hubbub will subside of its own accord. It always does. And I hope you'll agree that my harangue against the laxities of college security holds true.' He tapped the side of his nose. 'I might, in a roundabout way, have contributed to a heightened sense of future wariness.'

'By exposing a loophole in the system?' pre-empted Figueroa, features softening as she spoke.

Zolotov smiled his approval, and with it, his relief. The confession safely off his adrenalised mind, he was free to bask in her company.

'Our vinte minutos are up,' he enthused, signalling towards the bar. 'Let us drink to my speedy redemption.'

'Quite extravagant, Konstantin – even by your standards.'

'Extravagant yes, wasteful no. How can it be? The bottle was a gift.'

'Who from?'

'Really cannot say.'

'You mean you don't know, or you're choosing not to tell me?'

'Really cannot say,' he repeated in the same monotone.

Laughing hollowly at these ever more transparent attempts at evasion, Figueroa dwindled into silence. Luiz appeared on cue, silver tray in hand. Upon it stood two flutes, the chilled bottle of *Piper-Heidsieck* and an ice bucket. Asked how he wanted his bottle disgorged, Zolotov rasped: 'projectile method!'

He needn't have bothered.

Rather than catapulting across the low-ceilinged tier, the cork eased its way out with a sigh instead of a pop. Ignoring several ironic cheers from below, Luiz retrieved the fallen cork and placed it abashedly beside the ice bucket. Steadying a foam-splattered hand, he two-thirds filled each glass with champagne.

Zolotov brought his flute to his nose in a languid sweep. 'Bright, certainly bright, with floral top notes and even a hint of nougat . . . or is it caramel? Very nuanced indeed. Now for *your* oenological opinion, Rena. Not a frivolous exercise,' he added with a self-regarding frown, 'especially when one seeks a caviar lifestyle on a Pringles budget. You know, I really . . .'

Suddenly, his face blanched.

His tongue cleaved to his palate.

'*Stoj! Stoj!*'

The words were croaked, not shouted.

Figueroa arched a well-shaped eyebrow at her supervisor. For reasons soon to become apparent, Zolotov dashed the flute from her coral lips with a deft swipe of the hand. Striking the wooden table, it cracked sonorously at the rim, glissaded off the table's edge and shattered piercingly on the marble floor, sending shards of glass skimming across the surface. Thirty heads swivelled in alarm; but alarm soon heralded amusement as Zolotov held up a rueful, if dripping, hand.

'Tut, tut, Rena,' he sighed, soaking up the excess moisture with a napkin. 'Seems my praise was premature.' He would have continued to do so had he not beheld the horror emblazoned across her face. 'But you might,' he uttered with an unconvincing stab at *sang-froid*, 'be forgiven for recoiling at my behaviour.'

'I might *what*?' exclaimed Figueroa, as four waiters arrived with dustpans and brushes.

'I have – how shall I put this? – just saved your life. Wine I could understand, but there was always something sinister about champagne. Hence the unsigned note, I suppose.'

'Don't fuck me around, Konstantin! Tell me what the hell this is about, or I'm skedaddling.'

Zolotov loosened his watch strap by a single hole. 'You Argentines never *could* resist Americanisms. Simple geographical proximity, no? I have, Miss Figueroa, every reason to believe that our *Piper-Heidsieck* has been spiked: uncorked, poisoned, recorked.'

'Counterfeit?' she pumped, cheeks flushed with colour.

'No. The cork's distinctive mushroom shape suggests

that it's been in the bottle for years, not months. What is revealing, Rena, is Luiz's bungled attempt at disgorgement. The reduction in pressure from a *prior* uncorking resulted in less force being applied to the cork's base. Less force, so no pop.'

'Yes, but how do you recompress a cork into such a narrow mouth? Surely not manually.'

'With a pneumatic corking machine, of course. Like the one in Holdenby's lounge.'

'Looked more like an oversize stapler to me.'

He fixed her with a level stare. 'Just trust me on this one.'

'So how do you think it happened?'

'Think, Rena? Here's how I *know* it happened. The time is five-thirty, the date Friday the 9th of April. An expectant Holdenby melts into his leather recliner. He proceeds to delve into what he mistakenly assumes to be a saleable manuscript; money he dearly needs should the court case fall through. A man of literary stature, he recognises *The Kerensky Memoirs* within seconds. His mind is fraught with a mélange of fears: why is this Russian slimeball so conversant with the Olembé affair? Is he armed with more information than he would care to admit? Will he pursue the truth to its nauseating finale, not only jeopardising a lucrative lawsuit, but supplying evidence for two, three, perhaps four, life sentences? When he answers all these questions in the affirmative, it is then that I, Konstantin Zolotov, become fair game.'

'But how can you be sure that Holdenby sent the bottle?'

'Well ... we can rule out Fionnoula MacKenna for a start. Hard to imagine my tutorials being quite so dire. And it almost certainly didn't hail from Rae's wine-rack. Nothing there except entry-level *Moët et Chandon* and an unremarkable repertoire of clarets.'

Figueroa was irrepressible. 'But how did Holdenby know where to send it? You were going under a false name, remember? Even the email address you gave him was fake.'

'Patience, Rena. Only the other day, I found myself pillaging three filing cabinets for a hard copy of my iTunes Account Information. No success. Next, I emptied every one of my box-files. Similar story. Understand this: my Apple ID was listed as kzolotov@clapperton.ox.ac.uk, with my billing address directly below my payment information. My home address, Rena. Flat 17B, Tanley Court.'

'So you think your details became entangled in the ring-binder you gave Holdenby?'

'Almost certainly. Another stark reminder of my own fallibility.'

'Fallible or not, you intrigue me all the same.' Her tone occupied the awkward territory between raillery and admiration. 'It really wouldn't surprise me,' she rippled, as Zolotov shrugged his shoulders, 'if you'd mastered the art of spiked bottle detection as a toddler.'

The Russian leaned in closer. 'Let me make one thing perfectly clear,' he nasaled with an air of suppressed thunder. 'Zolotov does not, and will not, toddle. He may roam, skulk, saunter, peregrinate, prowl, amble, or indeed ramble, but never, *ever* does he toddle.' And with a disarming snort, he motioned towards the bar for what would prove to be a second Black Russian.

Figueroa contented herself with several snatched sips of her own creamy cocktail. When only ice remained, she succumbed to Zolotov's humourless, evaluating gaze.

'You know?' she uttered dreamily, shifting the position of her empty glass. 'Only this morning, I found myself completing a Postgraduate Research Questionnaire for the fifth time in as many years. Ticked all the usual boxes: 'is there appropriate financial support for research activities in the department?'– 'does the department provide sufficient scope for involvement in broader research culture?' – and my personal favourite: 'do the library facilities engender a climate of co-fraternity with those in your research community?' But my hand wavered over question four: 'Does your supervisor provide you with regular and constructive feedback on your progress?' She exhaled deeply. 'So what *do* you think of my performance? The perennial verve which goes unnoticed?'

Zolotov's face flickered to a smile. 'Your performance?' he rebounded, mimicking the fretful intonation in her voice. 'Your perennial verve? I might be better placed to answer these questions in the morning, think you not?'

Apologies and acknowledgements

Just for the record, there is no Cheltenham-based Lorenex Biotherapeutics. Never was, might never be. Albika plc, ARENSEFT Marketing and Trading, and Trás-os-Montes are no less imaginary. While all colleges are berthed in the wharf of reality, prudence required that their names were tweaked. All characters are fictitious, not least Professor Konstantin Vadimovich Zolotov, our outré protagonist. If she were real, (which I can assure you she isn't), Professor Dame Olsten would not deign to apologise for her scolding harangue against George Fawkins and 'God: A wishful mirage'. The inspiration behind Fawkins and his book is, I trust, instantly recognisable despite the thinly-veiled embellishments and odd letter substitution.

My sincere thanks to all of the below for their generosity of spirit.

Liz Salter and Charlie Ryan, whose Socratic questioning and informed encouragement convinced me to depart the well-trammelled path. Martin Dudley and James Trickey, who agreed to unconditional use of their Flickr photographs. I did, on deeper reflection, decide to reserve these for future projects, and have instead used 'Ebola' by Jason Merrill

Benedict as my cover motif. Many thanks to Jo Whelan for her *New Scientist* article entitled 'The viruses that kill tumours'. Anka Badowska, who unwittingly proved that the Latkey Online Transliteration Tool really *does* work. Liam O'Hara, Alex Goldsmith and Andrew Swampillai, whose positivity and sobering restraint were just the tonic throughout the conception stage. Finally, but by no means parenthetically, I owe an immense debt of gratitude to Ewa and Marek Kolczynski, the book's first readers and repositories of wisdom.

Glossary of Russian terms

- *Borzoi* – Also called the Russian Wolfhound, this silky-haired dog has long been a symbol of the landed gentry. A Borzoi's head is long, tapered and wedge-shaped.

- *Dorogaya moya* – Term of affection meaning 'my dear' or 'my darling', where the subject is female.

- *Gusli* – Russia's oldest plucked instrument. Wing-shaped or helmet-shaped, it has a distinctive zither-like timbre.

- *Jaleika* – A wind instrument from the western city of Tver, consisting of a barrel with finger holes and a flared bell. It utters a snuffling, plaintive sound – hardly surprising when its name is derived from the Russian word for pity.

- *Koryak* – An indigenous, reindeer-herding people from the northern part of the Kamchatka peninsula in the Russian Far East. Koryaks practice a shaman-centred form of animism based on the belief that the visible world is pervaded by spirits which affect the lives of the living.

Spiritual guide, soothsayer and healer, the shaman is seen as an intermediary between these two worlds.

- *Kubanskaya* – A vodka brand with a hint of lemon and honey. Anecdotal evidence would suggest that as vodkas go, Kubanskaya carries a relatively low hangover risk!

- *Medovukha* – Drunk by the Slavic Peoples since pagan times, Medovukha is a honey-based alcoholic beverage very similar to mead.

- *Psikhushka* – A colloquialism for psychiatric hospital. The Soviet authorities often used such institutions to isolate 'inconvenient' individuals from the rest of society, to break their will, and discredit their ideas. Western psychiatry at the time recognised but four types of schizophrenia: catatonic, hebephrenic, paranoid, and simple. 'Sluggish schizophrenia' was a concept pioneered by renowned psychiatrist Andrei Snezhnevsky, the diagnostic criteria for which were so vague that it could be applied to virtually anyone. In this way, it provided a pretext for the forcible hospitalisation of hundreds of sane political dissidents. 'Treatments' included electro-convulsive therapy interspersed with regular beatings, radiation torture and potent narcotics. If recent testimony is taken at face value, punitive psychiatry is not entirely gone from Russia.

- *Pyatizvyozdnaya* – Literally 'with five stars', this premium vodka is produced at the LIVIZ distillery in St. Petersburg.

- *Ni za chto!* – An exclamation meaning 'on no account!' or 'no way!'

- *Samizdat* – A term to describe the grassroots practice of underground publishing in the post-Stalin Soviet bloc. Typewritten texts with multiple carbon copies were compiled, the recipients of which retyped further copies and passed them along in chain-letter fashion. Literally 'self-published', the term has evolved to mean any attempt, anywhere in the world, in any medium, to evade official censorship.

- *Saratovskaya garmonika* – A uniquely Russian diatonic accordion, named after the southern city of Saratov. The instrument is configured to play the tonic major on the draw of the bellows, the reverse of a standard diatonic box. Bright and assertive, two integrated bells provide an unexpected, if somewhat irksome, rhythmic accompaniment.

- *S Rozhdestvóm!* – Short for '*Pozdravlyayu s Rozhdestvóm*', literally 'I congratulate you with Christmas'. The solitary 'S' is pronounced as a staccato hiss.

- *Tochka* – Full stop, both literally and figuratively.